'Hi, Abby,

A very deep,
her, and with
focussing imp
Abby's imagination involuntarily sprang into
action, images of a cool-suited sophisticate
leaping to mind. Perhaps there was another
young doctor Ross Bodey had forgotten to tell
her about!

'It's good to have you joining us.'

As the voice's hand gripped hers Abby
couldn't fail to be impressed by the strength
of its grip, and a smile played on the edge of
her lips as his image came into focus. Maybe
the Outback might have some advantages
after all!

Carol Marinelli is a nurse who loves writing. Or is she a writer who loves nursing? The truth is, Carol's having trouble deciding at the moment, but writing definitely seems to be taking precedence! She's happily married to an eternally patient husband and mother to three fabulously boisterous children. Add would-be tennis player, eternal romantic and devout daydreamer to the list and that pretty much sums Carol up. Oh, she's also terrible at housework!

Carol now also writes for Modern Romance™!

Recent titles by the same author:

Medical Romance™

THE BABY EMERGENCY
THE ELUSIVE CONSULTANT
THE SURGEON'S GIFT
EMERGENCY AT BAYSIDE

Modern Romance™

THE BILLIONAIRE'S CONTRACT BRIDE

THE BUSH DOCTOR'S CHALLENGE

BY
CAROL MARINELLI

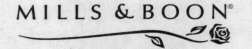

MILLS & BOON®

For Helen, Andy, Joshua and Louise
With love.

First published in Great Britain 2003
Harlequin Mills & Boon Limited,
Eton House, 18-24 Paradise Road, Richmond, Surrey TW9 1SR

© Carol Marinelli 2003

ISBN 0 263 83872 2

Set in Times Roman 10½ on 12 pt.
03-0104-48709

Printed and bound in Spain
by Litografia Rosés, S.A., Barcelona

CHAPTER ONE

'WHERE'S the airport?' Shouting her question over noise from the plane's engine, Abby was slightly taken back by the pilot's reaction when he started to chuckle. It hadn't been her intention to crack a joke!

'Show me a flat piece of land and I'll land this little lady!' Turning, Bruce grinned widely, showing rather too many gaps in his smile, and Abby forced a rather brittle one back, wishing he would turn his attention to the windscreen or whatever it was called on a plane and get on with flying the thing.

Her apparent aloofness for once had nothing to do with Abby's rather formal nature, for now it was borne of pure fear! The tiny plane that had met her on the tarmac of Adelaide airport seemed woefully inadequate for this long journey, and as they zipped through the late afternoon sky, as Abby struggled to concentrate on the mountain of paperwork in front of her, for the first time in ages there were only two questions buzzing through Abby's overactive mind. How the hell did this thing stay in the sky? And, perhaps more pointedly, how would anyone ever find them if it didn't?

'There's a flight strip near the clinic, we should be there in another fifteen minutes or so, give or take a few.'

'Thanks.'

Bruce's time frame was hardly rigid but, as Abby was fast learning, she might just as well have tossed her watch into the quarantine buckets when she'd left

Sydney. The same laid-back nature had been present in the ground staff who had greeted her when she'd landed tense and rushed at Adelaide, sure she was late for her connection. And when she'd finally located Bruce, standing by his plane, sipping on a cup of tea, he had assured Abby she had 'no worries'. Bruce, it would seem, would have been happy to wait all day for her if he had had to.

What have I taken on?

A third question was making itself heard as Abby gave up on the paperwork she was attempting to read and leant back in her seat, gazing at the red landscape beneath her. Mile upon endless mile stared back at her, like the coloured sands in the bottle in her small city kitchen back home. The rings of time indelibly etched on the landscape gaped beneath her, leaving Abby feeling as insignificant and as meaningless as the speck in the sky she surely was.

Mind you, it wasn't as if she'd had a choice but to take it on, Abby mused. Reece Davies, Director of Emergency, long-time colleague and supposed friend, had made his feelings on the subject pretty clear.

'There was nothing you could have done, Abby.'

How many times had he told her that? How many times had he pulled her into his office when Abby had ordered a multitude of tests on a patient for the most simple of complaints?

'Try telling that to the rest of the staff.'

'There's no need to tell them,' Reece had insisted. 'No one in this department thinks what happened that night was your fault.'

If only she could believe him, if only she could believe that the silence that descended every time Abby approached a clique of nurses had more to do with her seniority and less to do with David's death.

David.

A vague attempt at a smile inched across her lips as she tried to imagine David's take on all this. What David would say if he could see his Abby, the eternal city girl, on her way to three months in the middle of nowhere. But the start of a smile vanished as, once again, cruel realisation hit.

David was dead.

'So we're ordering abdominal ultrasounds on each and every abdominal pain now?' Reece's biting sarcasm as he'd audited her patient cards had hurt, but Abby had stood her ground, arguing it was surely far safer to err on the side of caution. To be sure, beyond any doubt, that her diagnosis was spot on.

But Reece had begged to differ.

'You need to get your confidence back, Abby,' he'd insisted. 'You need to regain some perspective. No one would have guessed Dave had a drug problem, no one.'

'Perhaps not, but if he hadn't been a friend, hadn't been a colleague, if David had just been a stranger wheeled through the doors, I'd have treated him differently.'

Reece had shaken his head, even offered his sympathies again for the terrible circumstances of that fateful night, but his stance had remained unchanged—if Abby wanted the upcoming consultant position in Emergency, then some grass roots medicine was the order of the day and Reece knew just the guy to teach her. And while she was at it, hell, why not go the whole hog and try making a couple of friends along the way?

'Back to grass roots—but, what grass?' Abby muttered to herself.

'Sorry, love? I didn't catch what you said.' Bruce turned again, his open face ready to join in the first conversation Abby had initiated, and Abby's blue eyes widened in angst, wishing Bruce would at least look as if he was controlling the plane!

'Nothing,' Abby shouted over the noise of the engine, embarrassed at being caught talking to herself. 'I was just saying that the land looks very dry.'

'Does it?' Bruce peered out of the side window for what seemed an inordinate length of time as Abby forcibly resisted the urge to take over the controls of the plane herself. 'No more than normal, love.'

Picking up her papers, Abby gave herself a mental shake. OK, so she was effectively out of action for three months, but you didn't have to be on the front line to fight a war. If her plans for the department were going to take shape then there was a pile of research to get through, people to be contacted, plans to be made. Her time in Tennengarrah wasn't going to be a total write-off.

She could still keep her promise to David...

As the very occasional buildings started to multiply, Bruce finally started to look at least a little like he was concentrating and Abby braced herself for a rather bumpy descent.

It never came. The only shudder she felt was when the plane touched down and a relieved escape of air came out of Abby's tense lips as they hurtled along the small landing strip.

'How was that, Doc?'

'Excellent!' Abby stood up, her first genuine smile of the day parting her full lips. Stretching her long legs, she plucked at some imaginary fluff on her very crisp, very white cotton shorts then ran a slightly anxious hand through her shock of long dark hair, wishing Bruce would stop grinning at her so she could touch up her lipstick.

'Here's Kell to meet you.'

'Kell?' Abby frowned as she hovered by the door. 'I thought Ross Bodey was supposed to be here.'

'Oh, sorry, I should have told you. Ross is on a call-out. I'll head off and pick him up soon, once I've had a cuppa.' Bruce didn't look sorry, not even remotely, and, picking up a large stainless-steel Thermos flask, he opened the exit door and jumped out easily before gallantly offering his hand as Abby made a rather more tentative descent to the dry soil beneath her. The low glare of the sun hitting her face on forced Abby's hand straight up to shield her eyes.

'Hi, Abby, I'm Kell.' A very deep, very masculine voice greeted her and with her sun-dazed eyes making focussing impossible for a moment or two, Abby's imagination involuntarily sprang into action, images of a cool, suited sophisticate springing to mind. Perhaps there was another young doctor Ross Bodey had forgotten to tell her about! 'It's good to have you joining us.' As the voice's hand gripped hers Abby couldn't fail to be impressed by the strength of its grip and a smile played on the edge of her lips as his image came into focus. Maybe the outback might have some advantages after all!

Wrong.

Never had a fantasy been so quickly dashed. Standing before her, smiling easily, was Mother Nature's original version of the Neanderthal man. A hulking brute of a male, well over six feet, was grinning down at her, dark shaggy black hair that needed a good cut hanging too far down his long thick neck, and dark eyes thickly rimmed with even darker lashes were smiling quizzically at her.

He wasn't wearing a loincloth exactly but the faded denim shorts he wore were a pretty good attempt, considering that was all he was wearing!

Even though Abby was wearing only white linen shorts and a crisp white blouse, coupled with some beige loafers, suddenly she felt terribly overdressed. 'Pleased to meet you,' Abby murmured, her eyes involuntarily travelling the long length of his impossibly tanned body, taking in the dark-haired legs and the chest hair, then blushing as she realised she'd been caught staring.

'Shelly wanted to come and meet you, but I told her to stay put, she's not feeling the best.'

'Is that right?' Pouring out a cup of tea from his well-loved Thermos then lighting up a cigarette, Bruce leant against the plane, obviously settling in for a chat. 'What's the problem?'

Abby fidgeted uncomfortably, anxious to get to the homestead, desperate to have a long cool shower as opposed to standing in forty degrees of heat for a cosy little chat.

'She's acting a bit strange.' Kell shrugged. 'So maybe you should hurry up your smoko and go and get Ross.'

Abby glanced over to Bruce, doubting anything short of a nuclear missile would hurry him up, but as Kell carried on chatting in his laid-back voice she did a double-take.

'If the baby is coming, Ross will want to be there.'

'She's in labour?' Abby gasped, but Kell just gave a vague shrug as Bruce noisily supped at his tea.

'Well, Shelly insists she isn't, but if you ask me she isn't far off. She's been cleaning like a woman possessed this morning, and now she's pacing up and down like a tractor turning the soil.'

'And from that you assume she's in labour?' There was a slightly sarcastic edge to Abby's voice, which she quickly fought to correct. After all, it wasn't Kell's fault he didn't know what he was talking about!

'I'm just saying I'd be happier if Ross was here, and that as much as Shelly refuses to admit it, I think she'd be happier, too,' Kell added, with all the authority of a man who'd no doubt single-handedly delivered a zillion calves! 'She's supposed to be flown to Adelaide in the morning.'

'When's she due?' Bruce asked, slurping his drink in such a disgusting fashion Abby felt like putting her hands up to her ears.

'Three weeks tomorrow, but they'll take her to Adelaide in case the baby comes early.'

'Do all pregnant women go to Adelaide?' Abby asked, curiosity getting the better of her. Though she only half listened to the answer, sure these two bush buddies wouldn't have a clue about maternity arrangements.

'Just the complicated ones.' Kell gave a knowing nod and Bruce scratched his head.

'It's upside down, isn't it?'

'Breech,' Abby said, trying to keep the note of superiority out of her voice. 'She probably won't need a Caesarean section, but it's better to be on the safe side. Breech deliveries can be complicated.'

'Is that right? Rightio, then.' Taking his cue, Bruce threw the dregs of his drink onto the ground and took another moment or two to replace his lid and cup. 'I'd better step on it. Will you be all right? I mean, if Shelly really is about to have the little tacker, do you want me to give anyone a call?'

'Good idea,' Abby said approvingly, then snapped her mouth closed as Kell overrode her.

'Oh, we'll be right.' Kell shrugged again. 'But more to the point, Shelly will kill me if I go summoning the troops. I'll catch you later, then, Bruce.' As Kell turned to go Abby stood there bemused for a moment before calling him. 'What about my luggage?'

'Bruce will bring it in later when he drops Ross back. I've only got the bike.' Gesturing to a massive brute of a motorcycle parked in the middle of nowhere, he didn't seem to notice or, more pointedly, chose to ignore Abby's gasp of horror.

'But my computer…' Her voice trailed off as Kell gave her a curious look.

'It will be fine. Bruce will only be gone an hour or so. No one's going to take it.'

Maybe not, but if Bruce went and fell asleep at the controls, which Abby reasoned wouldn't exactly be far off from where he was now, not only would all her drug rehab research go up the shoot, she'd be stuck in this God-forsaken place without the internet, and heaven forbid, the chance to email every last one of her family to tell them about the worst career move in history.

'I'd like my computer, please.' Standing her ground, Abby watched as Kell gave her another quizzical look, combined with another brief shrug.

'Whatever you say. Hey, Bruce!'

Ambling his way over, Abby watched as the two men exchanged a few words, no doubt moaning about the little princess who needed all her gadgets. Well, let them moan, Abby thought fiercely, she needed her computer, it wasn't exactly a big thing to ask!

'Here you go.' Handing her the black bag, Abby

mumbled her thanks, her eyes travelling behind him to the large white building.

'The clinic's bigger than I thought.'

That was the understatement of the millennium. For weeks now Abby had been having visions of a tiny tin shack, with a rickety sign bearing a red cross on the outside. Maybe it was the word 'clinic' that had caused her misconception, conjuring up images of a halfway house, a holding bay until *real* help arrived, but the very white, very large building she was looking at now looked suspiciously like a hospital.

Kell nodded as Abby carried on staring. 'It's getting there. Half of it is still under construction, but it's coming along. I'd take you round for a quick tour, but Ross asked me to keep an eye on Shelly. I can take you in, though. Clara's on duty, she'll be only too happy to show you around.'

'That's fine,' Abby said quickly, suddenly overcome with nerves at the prospect of meeting everyone. 'I'll wait for the doctor.' Her words came out horribly wrong, superior and condescending, but thankfully Kell didn't respond, just climbed on the bike. It wasn't as if he'd be up on the intricacies of hospital hierarchy to be offended by her words, Abby consoled herself, making a mental note to be a bit more diplomatic.

'Do you want me to hold your computer for you?' Kell volunteered as Abby eyed the bike suspiciously and lifted one very wary leg. 'Would that make things easier?'

'Thanks.' He slipped the carry strap over his shoulder and waited patiently, a slight grin on his lips as Abby struggled to mount, her cheeks still burning from the mess she had made of his polite offer to introduce her. But it wasn't only embarrassment and the thought of climbing on the brute of a thing that was giving Abby palpitations, it was the realisation that she had no hope of getting on, straddling the thing and riding the couple of kilometres or so to the homestead without touching Kell. Or more pointedly, without touching the vast expanse of naked skin that she simply couldn't seem to tear her eyes away from.

She wanted to ask him for a helmet, to point out the dangers of riding a bike without one. How dammed irresponsible they were being and how awful it would look in her obituary if an emergency doctor was killed riding a bike without one.

But what would be the point?

All that would achieve would be to make her look even more neurotic. Still, if this was how they got about here, she was going to make damned sure she bought one for herself, order one from the internet if she had to.

At least she had her computer.

'Whoops.' Midway through starting the engine, he stopped. Climbing off, Kell opened the back box Abby was leaning on and took out two of the offending objects. 'Better to be safe. Ross would never forgive me if I killed the new doctor on her first day here.'

The annoying thing was, now that she'd got what she'd only seconds ago wanted, Abby had no idea what to do with the blessed thing. Oh, she could get it on, and hopefully it was the right way around, but the straps on Kell's helmet had clipped together easily, whereas hers…

'Here.' He was standing next to her, clipping together the connection and tightening the straps under her chin. As unwashed and unkempt as he looked, this close up Abby realised it just wasn't the case as she caught the faint scent of his soap mingling with a strong masculine deodorant that most definitely did the job. As he lifted his arms and fitted her helmet, pulling the straps so taut under her chin Abby was sure she might choke, the worst part of it all was that while she suffered this brief indignation there was no place else to look than at his very flat, very brown stomach.

OK, he was sexy, Abby admitted reluctantly, in a sort of overgrown, salt-of-the-earth way.

Very sexy, she conceded, eyes level with his epicentre. Even his belly button was sexy, which up to this point Abby had been sure was an impossible feat. Belly buttons were just that—belly buttons. But Kell's, well, the hair around it circled gently, and Abby found herself momentarily mesmerised by the strange beauty of such a normally nondescript object.

'Third time lucky.' Kell grinned, climbing nimbly in front of her and shouting over his shoulder as the bike sprang into life between her thighs. 'Let's go.'

Abby had never been on a motorbike in her life. In fact, she'd barely graduated to getting the training wheels taken off her push bike before books had beckoned, or a drop of pond water placed under her father's antiquated microscope had held more excitement than riding around the back garden in circles. And now here she was in the middle of nowhere, roaring along a dusty red road clinging on for dear life to a man she'd only just met.

It was terrifying, exhilarating and strangely... Abby's mind clicked over, struggling against the whipping hair around her face to find the word she was looking for.

Sexy.

There it was again.

Thousands of dollars' worth of chrome catapulting

them along the rough, unsealed road, and it would be a lie by omission not to recognise the added thrill of Kell's snaky hips beneath her hands, her fingers coiling through the loops on his shorts, and unless she wanted to fall off the palms of her hand had nowhere else to go other than resting on his warm, bronzed skin. Abby kept her body well back, though, leaning against the back box, terrified she might be catapulted forward and forced to touch more of him.

It was over too soon, and vague memories of the waltzers at the fairground surfaced as Abby took Kell's hand and attempted to dismount with at least a shred of dignity. Her legs felt as if they didn't quite know what to do and the ground still seemed to be moving.

'Sorry.' Kell grinned. 'I didn't realise it was your first time, you should have told me.'

'Why?' Abby shrugged. 'Would you have treated me more gently?'

Ouch! The sexual connotation had never been intended, and as Kell grinned ever wider Abby followed him up the steps of a massive house, wondering where her attempt at flirting had blown in from.

Yes, he was sexy, yes, he was a fine specimen of a man and all that, but a farm labourer with a thing about bikes certainly wasn't on Abby's agenda.

She was here to work.

Three months of grass roots medicine and she was out of here, and if Bruce's plane collapsed, no matter, she'd walk if she had to.

'Abby!' A very pregnant, very pretty, red-headed woman came out of a fly door and stood at the top of the steps, the massive laundry basket she was carrying in no way covering up the enormous swell of the baby within her. 'I'm Shelly, we spoke briefly on the telephone. I'm so sorry Ross isn't here to meet you.'

'That's no problem.' Abby smiled in what she hoped was a friendly fashion. 'Kell made me very welcome.'

'Did I?' Kell asked with a vaguely surprised grin. 'I wasn't even trying.'

'I was being polite,' Abby muttered, as Kell's grin widened.

'Tell you what, come to the watering hole with me tonight and meet the locals, we'll show you a real Tennengarrah welcome. I'll even leave the bike at home this time.'

'I might just give it a miss, thanks.'

Even though his offer had been imparted in his usual laid-back style, Abby couldn't help but feel a flurry of butterflies as she said no. OK, he wasn't exactly asking her out on a date, but it was certainly the closest Abby had come in a long time.

A very long time.

'You should go,' Shelly pushed happily. 'If I wasn't the size of a baby elephant, I'd take you there myself.' Putting the basket down, Shelly rubbed her back and gave a weary smile. 'Come inside. We'll have a drink and then I'll take you over to where you'll be staying— it's that one.' She pointed over to any one of about three white houses scattered on the perimeter of the property. 'It's all ready for you.'

Privately all Abby wanted to do was grab the keys and head off but, not wanting to be appear rude, she smiled appreciatively and followed a rather cumbersome Shelly back up the steps, hesitating slightly as she realised Kell was joining them.

'Kell,' Shelly said as he followed them in. 'You don't

have to babysit me. I've got Abby here now, she *is* a doctor.'

'I'm not babysitting,' Kell insisted, but Shelly shook her head.

'So why have you spent the whole afternoon painting the baby's nursery when Ross was going to do it at the weekend?'

'When did Ross ever get a weekend off?' Kell said, collapsing onto the couch and placing two massive feet onto the coffee-table before him, which had Abby cringing, though Shelly didn't seem remotely bothered. 'Anyway, I need the cash.'

For some reason Shelly seemed to find this hilarious and picking up a T-shirt she tossed it in Kell's vague direction. 'Well, if you're staying you can at least put some clothes on.

'Kell thought I needed a rest,' Shelly explained to a politely smiling Abby. 'So he decided to make lunch.'

'You don't have to tell everyone,' Kell grumbled, pulling a very white T-shirt over his head, much to Abby's relief. Now at least she'd be able to look at him without blushing. 'Trouble is he ended up wearing a bottle of mayonnaise.'

'It's not my fault Ross screws the lids on so tight.' He cast a brief look to Abby. 'I don't usually walk around half-naked. Sorry if I scared you.' Fortunately, Abby was saved from answering as he turned back to Shelly. 'Look, if you really don't want me around I'll head off, but I think I've at least earned a cup of coffee.'

Which, Abby reasoned, at the rate Shelly was moving, would probably give Bruce plenty of time to have Ross safely back home. This man took his duties seriously.

'Abby, would you like a coffee?'

'Thanks.' Abby smiled. 'If you show me where things are I'll make it. You look as if you're a bit busy.'

'Just a bit,' Shelly admitted, gesturing to the mountains of laundry adorning every available surface. 'I'll feel so much better when all this is done.'

Abby chose to ignore Kell's upwardly mobile right eyebrow as she fumbled around the kitchen, watching with undisguised bemusement as Shelly proceeded to tear the wrappers off a pile of new baby clothes and bundle them into yet another laundry basket.

'So how was the journey, Abby?'

'Long.'

Shelly laughed. 'Tell me about it. I remember the first time I came here I thought the journey would never end. It's like another planet, isn't it?'

Abby nodded, her smile finally genuine as she warmed to the likable Shelly.

'Hard to believe it's the same country. Just wait till Ross takes you out and you see some of the homesteads, miles and miles from anywhere. They make Tennengarrah look like a thriving city—at least we've got a pub and a few shops, and a hairdresser's…'

'Since when?' Kell asked, perking up a bit and leaning forward.

'Well, not a hairdresser's exactly,' Shelly conceded. 'But June Hegley's niece, Anna, is staying for a few months and apparently she trained in Sydney, so she's going to set up shop at June's house.'

'I must remember to make an appointment,' Kell said, shooting a wink at Abby, who realised with a start she was again staring at him.

That shaggy dark mane that framed his face could certainly do with a cut, but on the other hand it actually suited him, Abby couldn't quite imagine Kell with the short back and sides which was so much part of the uniform of most of her colleagues.

'The clinic's nice,' Shelly chattered on, happily oblivious to the sudden crackling tension in the room. 'It's really come a long way since we've been here. I think you'll be quite pleasantly surprised.'

'How busy does it get?'

Her question was aimed at Shelly. From their brief chats on the telephone and a couple of longer ones with Ross, Abby had gleaned that Shelly was a nurse who until recently had been working, but Kell, who obviously thought he knew everything about anything, decided to answer for her.

'All depends. Sometimes you can go a full day without even getting a new patient, but those days are getting few and far between now. With tourism and everything the town's thriving.'

Sucking in her breath, Abby bit back a smart answer, her eyes pointedly trained on Shelly. 'So, how long have you been here?'

'Just over a year. It took me a while to settle in but I think I'm finally getting the hang of it. Matthew, on the other hand, fell in love the first day he was here.'

'Matthew's Shelly's son,' Kell interrupted needlessly, and Abby didn't even bother to answer him, again directly addressing Shelly.

'How old's Matthew?'

'Three. He'll be up soon, he's just having an afternoon nap, which is great for me as I finally got a parcel today. Mum sent me some baby clothes and a few odds and ends.' Holding up a box of laundry powder, Shelly grinned. 'You'd be surprised the things you miss.'

'They don't sell laundry powder here?' Abby asked, aghast, visions of washing her shorts with a rock in the creek gushing into her mind. What on earth had she let herself in for?

'What's laundry powder?'

It took a second for Abby to register Kell was joking. Blushing, she took another drink as Shelly started to laugh. 'It's not that bad, Abby. I wanted some soap flakes, but the local shop didn't quite stretch, so it was quicker to get Mum to send some than wait till we do our big shop in town next month. Now, if you two don't mind, I'll just go and throw this lot in the washing machine.'

'Go ahead.' Kell nodded, flicking on the television with the remote. 'I'll go and get the other basket pegged out for you.'

Abby tried, she really did. She tried not to roll her eyes but sitting in the middle of nowhere discussing the merits of soap flakes versus detergent was just so far removed from her normal life she couldn't help herself.

'Something wrong?' Kell asked.

'Nothing,' Abby retorted.

'Shelly's great,' Kell enthused. 'And if the conversation's not up to your usual standards, bear in mind the poor woman's about to give birth.'

'I didn't say anything,' Abby protested, annoyed with herself for being caught out, and also irritated with Kell for his uneducated assumptions. Shelly Bodey did not look like a woman about to give birth!

'You didn't have to.'

They sat in uncomfortable silence for a moment or two before Abby succumbed, curiosity finally the getting the better of her. 'Kell, why is she washing new clothes?'

'You're supposed to wash them,' Kell explained patiently, his smile back in place to show her she was forgiven, 'before the baby wears them. It gets rid of any perfume or harsh detergents.'

To Abby's utter surprise she found she was actually laughing.

'What did I say?'

'Nothing.' Taking a sip of her coffee, Abby started to laugh again then forced herself to stop. 'It's just the last thing I expected to hear from a guy like you.'

'A guy like me?' Kell asked as he stood up and picked up the laundry basket. 'What, do you think I'm too macho to know about washing powders and the like?'

Finally she managed to look at him. It should have been so much easier now he was wearing clothes, but even without visual access to that toned body he was still stunning, and something about the way he was looking at Abby had her stomach doing somersaults. He looked so ridiculously gorgeous, six feet five of oozing masculinity with a laundry basket tucked under his arm and a handful of pegs!

'You'd better get on.' Abby smiled. 'If you want to get your washing dry.'

It was Kell laughing this time. 'Now, what would a woman like you know about laundry?'

As the fly door slammed Abby let out a long-held breath and sank back into the deep sofa, staring out of the window, her gaze filtering out the so-called town to the view beyond which seemed to stretch on to infinity. Mile after mile of red soil, no bay view, no skyscrapers, no hum of traffic in the distance, just the aching gap of emptiness. Staring moodily out as the sun bobbed lower in the sky, Abby truly wondered how she could possibly survive.

Three months, she consoled herself.

In three short months she'd be handing her washing over at the dry-cleaners without even meriting it a thought.

In three months she'd be a consultant.

CHAPTER TWO

'KELL!'

Shelly's voice wasn't particularly loud, but the note of urgency in it had Abby on her feet in less than a second.

'Kell!' Shelly's voice was louder this time, more desperate. Putting down her mug, Abby cast an anxious look through the window, catching sight of an oblivious Kell, happily pegging out the washing, his mouth full with pink plastic pegs.

Unsure whether to call Kell or investigate herself, Abby tentatively followed the sound of Shelly's increasingly urgent demands. As she pushed open the laundry door, she swallowed a gasp of shock as Shelly let out a deep guttural groan, two frightened eyes darting up to meet Abby's as she hunched over the washing machine.

'I want to push!'

Please, don't. Abby didn't say it, but she definitely thought it!

Stay calm. Abby mentally steadied herself making her way over and gently helping a groaning Shelly onto the floor. *There's a clinic two minutes away filled with nurses, equipment…* Her mind flashed to her doctor's bag winging its way across the outback, a doctor's bag with artery forceps and umbilical clamps and, luxury of luxury, latex gloves. For that split second she could have cheerfully strangled Kell with her bare hands.

'I'll get Kell to ring the clinic,' Abby said assuredly, pushing herself up from the floor, but Shelly's hand

24

grabbed her arm as she shook her head, her face purple as she started to bear down.

'It's coming now!'

'Then we'd better get on and deliver this baby' Abby soothed, her voice amazingly calm given her rapid heart rate. 'We'll manage just fine.'

Grabbing a handful of folded towels, Abby took a deep steadying breath. She hadn't delivered a baby for years.

Years!

Even then it had only been a token attempt, with registrars and midwives beside her in a delivery room packed with equipment! Still, she reassured herself, fast labours were normally easy, just a steadying hand to help Mother Nature along. But as she examined Shelly Abby's heart sank and Shelly's question reiterated Abby's findings from her brief assessment.

'Is the baby still breech?'

'Yes,' Abby's said, in what she prayed was a confident voice, as Shelly let out a moan of terror.

'I thought it had turned. I said to Ross this morning—'

'Shelly,' Abby broke in firmly, 'the baby's going to be fine. I just need you to listen carefully to what I'm telling you to do.' Her eyes shot up to her new patient and she forced a smile. 'I'm going to shout for Kell. He can get someone over with a delivery pack, so try not to push just yet.'

'What if I can't stop myself?'

Abby took a deep steadying breath then looked up at Shelly, her smile every inch the confident emergency doctor she was. 'Then we'll deal with it.'

'Kell!'

It wasn't exactly a dulcet summons but, given that the television was still blaring and no doubt he was still playing housemaid, Abby wasn't exactly left with much choice.

'What's up?'

He strolled into the laundry and to Abby's bemusement he didn't even look remotely fazed by the sight that greeted him.

'Ring the clinic,' Abby said through gritted teeth, as the baby's buttocks descended lower in the birth canal, Shelly's agonised screams splitting the hot afternoon air like a knife.

He returned moments later, pulling open a large leather bag, and Abby nodded her thanks as he handed her a pair of gloves and started to open a large paper-wrapped pack. 'Did you ring?'

'Yep, Clara's on standby' Kell said as Abby's eyes widened in horror.

'I don't want Clara to be on standby,' she hissed as loudly as she could without alarming Shelly. 'I want her to send a team.' Hell, why didn't this Neanderthal just do as she asked? Yes, she was a doctor but this was a complicated delivery. Beads of sweat were on her brow as she struggled to stay calm. Why was Kell still here? Shouldn't he do the polite thing and go and boil some water or something?

'I've got to push,' Shelly begged, and as the baby moved further down the birth canal Abby wasn't sure what terrified her the most—the thought of a breech birth with no back-up or the fact Kell was pulling on a pair of gloves.

'We are the team, Abby,' Kell said in low tones, bending down so that only she could hear. 'This as good as it gets here.' His voice changed then, coming out lighter and friendly, as he looked up and smiled at Shelly. 'The little one's still bottoms up, Shelly, so I'm just going to move you.'

To Abby's stunned amazement, in one quick motion he scooped Shelly up as easily as if she were a child and deposited her gently on the laundry bench. Then, pulling a basket over, he kicked it upside down and pushed Abby's shoulders firmly down till she was sitting. As the fog cleared from her shell-shocked brain Abby realised Shelly was actually in the perfect position for a breech delivery.

'You're a nurse?' Abby muttered, as the baby edged ever closer.

'And a midwife,' Kell whispered, guiding her hand to take the weight of the buttocks now being delivered.

'You never said.'

'You never asked.'

There wasn't time for a smart reply. Shelly started to groan in earnest now, her frightened screams filling the small laundry. 'I want Ross!'

'He'll be here soon, Shelly.' Kell's smile was far more effortless and, Abby realised, far more reassuring than hers.

'I wanted him to be here!' Shelly's voice was rising as another contraction gripped her, and with a grunt that defied her tiny frame she bore down, but seemed to change her mind halfway, her arms flailing in agony, panic overwhelming her. Breech deliveries required a supreme maternal effort combined with concentration and Abby looked up anxiously, worried by Shelly's lack of focus, knowing she needed her onside here.

'Shelly, listen to me…' Abby started, but a warm hand on her shoulder halted her in mid-sentence and she briefly turned her anxious eyes to Kell, who nodded assuredly.

'She'll be fine,' he mouthed, then turned his attention to the restless woman. 'Shelly, Ross is on his way, and we all know how much you need him right now, but holding back until he gets here isn't the right thing to do. This little one isn't waiting for anyone, so you need to do what Abby says and stay with us, OK?'

There was an air of authority in his laid-back voice, an assurity that to this point had been missing from the room, and Shelly responded to it.

'I'm just scared.'

'Why?' Kell asked easily. 'Abby's got it all covered. You and the baby are both going to be fine.'

There was a strange pecking order in medicine. The fact Abby was a doctor supposedly overrode Kell, and, given that she had started the delivery, if Kell were to rush in and take over it could, by some, be seen as professional discourtesy. But at that moment Abby would have very happily given up her seat on the upturned basket and willingly handed the reins to a far more experienced midwife. This was not the welcome she had expected, and Abby took a deep, calming breath trying to quell the mounting panic inside her before the next contraction came and they set to work again.

'All right?' Kell checked, and Abby felt both embarrassed and strangely pleased that he seemed to sense her trepidation.

'I hope so,' Abby mouthed, and then suddenly it was her turn to benefit from his rather dazzling smile.

'You'll be fine, too,' he said quietly as Shelly pushed for all she was worth as Abby and Kell shouted encouragement. With the lower trunk of the baby delivered, Shelly had a welcome break for a moment or two, but there was no time for Abby to relax. She checked a loop of the cord and nodded to Kell, the steady pulsing of the cord reassuring her that the baby wasn't in distress, but she had the shoulders to deal with next and then the hardest part, the head.

'OK, let's go.' Kell sounded as enthusiastic as he had when he'd started his bike as the next contraction started.

Abby felt a surge of confidence. Surely if Kell wasn't worried she must be doing OK. One strong hand assisted her, gently pushing Abby's hand, guiding her to deliver the baby's shoulder downwards towards the floor. Suddenly Abby felt in control, the textbooks, the deliveries she had observed springing into her mind like a much-watched video. The shoulders were out now and she cast a quick glance up to Kell.

'Hold steady a moment, Shelly.' Coming round to Abby, he guided her arm to the infant, so that the baby was effectively straddling Abby's forearm with its arms and legs. 'Just let it hang for a moment,' Kell said gently, and Abby gave a grateful nod, the weight of the baby allowing gravity to help with the delivery of its head. His hand was back on hers now, guiding her middle finger into the infant's mouth as Abby used her other hand to increase the flexion of the head.

She drew the body of the babe first downward and then forward, the baby over Shelly's abdomen as the last inches of the birth canal were negotiated, until finally, with a relief that literally overwhelmed Abby, the head was out, the baby was out and safe, taking a huge breath, its little eyes blinking in indignation as it was delivered. Abby placed the slippery bundle on Shelly's stomach, whose hands moved down to scoop the babe up to her, tears streaming down her face as Kell rubbed the stunned little baby vigorously with a towel.

'A little girl,' she gasped. 'I've got a little girl.'

'A beautiful little girl, too.' Kell's words were coming

out almost as choked as Shelly's and to Abby's amazement she watched as a sparkle of tears flashed in his dark eyes. 'Look how blonde she is—she's her father's daughter all right.'

'And she's OK?'

Better than OK. One little girl was pinking up before their very eyes as Kell continued to rub, her dark red lips parted to allow a furious scream to escape.

As Kell dashed off to find a duvet Abby clamped and cut the cord, the placenta delivering with satisfying ease. Wrapping a bundle of towels around the baby and a large bath sheet around a shivering Shelly, she stood for a moment, just revelling in the sheer and utter miracle of birth.

'Abby.' Kell was at the door, only his face peering around as he pushed the duvet through the gap. 'Cover Shelly up, I've got a little guy here who's woken up with a bit of a fright.'

'Matthew?' Shelly gasped, tearing her eyes away from her newborn as Abby quickly tucked the duvet around the pair. 'He must be terrified.'

'He'll be fine,' Abby said assuredly, but Shelly begged to differ.

'He won't understand.' Her eyes met Abby's. '*You* don't understand. Matthew's got Down's syndrome. Ross and I had planned how we were going to introduce him. I was supposed to be in bed, the baby in a crib, Ross was going to—'

'Do you want me to help you into the bedroom, get you settled a bit before he sees you?'

Shelly shook her head. 'He's awake now, you'd better just tell Kell to bring him in.'

Abby nodded and, doing a quick check to make sure

there was nothing that might scare Matthew, she went to open the laundry door.

'Abby.' Turning, Abby smiled at Shelly, her hand on the doorhandle. 'Would you hold her for me? It might make things a bit...' Her voice trailed off and Abby stood there, looking at the mother cradling the daughter she had just delivered, and suddenly the lump that had been missing in her throat till now was so big it threatened to choke her.

'I'd be glad to.'

A mother's love...

Taking the swaddled bundle, Abby stared into the most innocent of all faces. Every fibre in Shelly's being would be telling her she should be holding her baby, and yet a deep maternal instinct also told her that a little guy needed her now. Needed his mum to hold her arms out to him, to tell him what had taken place while he'd quietly slept.

Carefully holding the baby close, Abby pulled open the laundry door.

Two blue eyes met hers, two blue bewildered little eyes in a sleep-crumpled face.

'This is Abby, Matty,' Kell crooned gently. 'She's Tennengarrah's new doctor.' Wisely Kell didn't acknowledge the baby Abby was holding, leaving that introduction to Shelly.

'Matthew.' Shelly's arms were outstretched, her tired face managing a bright smile, her voice, her attention, all focussed on her son. 'Did you get a fright, sweetheart?'

He didn't say anything, just nodded seriously as Kell carefully passed him to his mother. 'There's nothing to be scared of Matthew. Abby and Kell have been looking after Mummy, and look who's finally here.'

Taking her cue, Abby stepped forward, holding the infant where her big brother could get a proper look, and the lump in her throat swelled like bread in water as Matthew peered into the swaddle of towel.

'Baby.' His little face broke into a smile that met each ear and the whole room seemed to relax a notch, the tension seeping out as two inquisitive eyes searched his new sister's face. 'My baby!' Matthew squealed excitedly.

'That's right big guy, it's your baby sister.' Kell laughed, one eye on Matthew, the other on a wilting Shelly. Scooping Matthew out of a tired Shelly's arms, he held the little boy closer, allowing him to touch the tiny face. 'That's right, don't touch her eyes, and just give her little cheek a stroke. I'll bet she can't wait for you to give her a big cuddle, but do you know what, little guy? First we have to get Mummy into bed, and I'm gonna need a hand. Do you think you can help me?'

Put like that, how could Matthew refuse?

Somehow, in a matter of minutes Kell had them organised. A now over-excited Matthew turned back the sheets on the bed and plumped pillows as Kell guided a very wobbly Shelly to the main bedroom. Abby followed, carrying the newborn as carefully as if she were the crown jewels, staring down into that tiny wide-eyed face, unable to believe the feelings this ten-minute-old baby was unleashing.

Oh, Abby had held babies before, well, sort of. She'd examined more tiny chests than most people had had cooked dinners, probed more little abdomens than she cared to remember, even bounced the odd baby or two on her knee during her time on the children's ward.

But to hold one so new, so close and for so long was doing the strangest things to her.

To know that unaided by a huge team, she had brought this wanted, precious life into the world suddenly made that medical degree seem a touch more personal.

'You were great.' Kell was sitting on the bed and Abby did a double take when she stepped in the bedroom. 'Shelly's just in the loo,' he explained, patting the bed beside him.

'I only did great thanks to you,' Abby admitted, not even bothering to look up. The face of the baby held far too much appeal.

But then again...her eyes flicked up and they were met by Kell's black, coal chips.

'I was just giving myself a big pat on the back about how well I'd done, but I'm the first to admit that I nearly had a full-scale panic attack when I saw the baby was breech. Heaven only knows what would have happened if you hadn't been there.'

'It would have been exactly the same,' Kell said with the same assurance he had used with Shelly. 'A couple of minutes of internal panic and it would have all clicked. You know that as well as I do.'

'I hope so. Were you even a little bit worried?'

'No, I never worry.' Abby gave him a disbelieving look but Kell just stood up and rapped on the *en suite* door. 'Are you all right, Shelly?'

'A couple more minutes,' came the distant reply, and Kell frowned.

'Don't you go fainting on me now, Shelly. Two more minutes or I'll come in and fetch you myself.' Smiling, he came back from the door. 'Hey, Matty, why don't you go and get a toy for the baby to put in her cot?' As Matthew scampered off, Kell sat back down. 'I hope she's all right in there.'

'This is the man who less than a minute ago told me he never worried.'

Kell laughed, but just as he opened his mouth to speak the bedroom door was flung open and they both turned as a tall blond man burst in.

'Where's Shelly?'

It was a strange way to meet your new colleague, strange but definitely not awkward or difficult. As Abby stood up Ross Bodey's jaw literally dropped, an incredulous look on his face as his eyes locked on the baby Abby held.

'Who's this?' he choked, as Abby stood there, speechless.

'Are you talking about the gorgeous raven, or the ravishing redhead?' Kell quipped, but his voice was thick with emotion as the bathroom door opened and a pale-looking Shelly tentatively stepped out.

'I'm talking about the blonde,' Ross said slowly, one arm pulling his wife towards him as he shakingly took the baby from Abby.

'I'm sorry,' Shelly sobbed, the emotion of the evening finally catching up. 'I tried to hold on.'

'There's absolutely nothing to be sorry for.' His eyes never left his daughter as he gently led his wife to the bed. 'This is the best homecoming I've ever had.'

'*Wun.*' Matthew was at the door now. Charging in, he placed a battered book in the crib, his face splitting in two as he saw Ross sitting on the bed.

'Hey, buddy, don't I get a kiss?'

'Daddy!'

'I think we might have outstayed our welcome,' Kell whispered to Abby. 'How about you let me buy you that drink now?'

'How about you show me where I can have a shower?'

They said their goodbyes, an engrossed Ross attempting to apologise for landing Abby in it, but his mind was clearly on the latest addition to his family.

'Abby will be fine.' Kell grinned. 'I'll bring her luggage over and show her around. Don't worry about a thing, just enjoy tonight.'

'No problem there,' Ross said, then turned to Abby. 'Look, thank you, I really mean that.'

'It was a pleasure,' Abby said warmly. Stepping out into the now dark sky, a billion stars twinkling down, the warm hand of Kell guiding her along the dusty red soil, it hit her, a heady mixture of relief at what had transpired and utter fear at how different the scenario could have been.

'You're crying?' His voice was questioning, concerned, but not for a second mocking.

'I know.' Abby sniffed loudly as she fished in her pockets for a handkerchief. 'It's never got to me like that—a birth, I mean. It's always been nice, special.' The words were buzzing in her head as Abby attempted to articulate the strange emotions that were assailing her. 'But at the end of the day it's been a job well done. Tonight it just got to me. Seeing Matthew, he was so cute, bringing the baby his book, and then Ross...' Another tear splashed down her cheek and Abby wiped it away then gave in as a few more followed. 'He was so thrilled, so delighted with his new daughter, yet he still managed to make Matthew feel number one.'

As Abby started to walk again, Kell pulled her back. 'You think that's a tear-jerker?' His eyes were searching hers as Abby's returned his stare. 'Wait till you hear this—Matthew isn't Ross's son.'

He watched as Abby's lips parted, as the tears started spilling again.

'They've only been married a year, and you know what? He loves that little guy as if he was his own. That's love for you.'

'She's a lucky woman,' Abby said slowly, but Kell shook his head.

'They're all lucky.' Taking her hand, he led her along the pathway. 'They found each other.'

'This is you.'

Pushing open the unlocked door, Kell stood back and let Abby into her new home.

Her luggage lay higgledy-piggledy on the dark wooden floor, no doubt courtesy of Bruce, and Abby stood a moment as Kell flicked on the light.

'It's pretty basic. Kitchen.' He gestured ahead. 'Lounge.' Stomping along the hallway, he flicked on another light and Abby was somewhat surprised to find herself standing in a beautifully furnished room. A large wooden fan whirred away overhead bouncing a shadow off the white walls, broken by vast Aboriginal paintings, the native art so much more appropriate in its own setting than the museums Abby was used to seeing it in. The soft-cushioned cane furnishing looked inviting and the huge low table in the middle of the large room would be the perfect spot for her computer.

'Oh.'

'What's wrong?'

'I left my computer back at Ross and Shelly's.'

'Well, I'm not going back to get it,' Kell said quickly. 'That's one little party I'm not breaking up.'

'Of course not,' Abby snapped, kicking herself for even mentioning it. 'I was just saying.'

'So we're back where we started?' Kell turned to her. 'Arguing about a computer.'

'Nobody's arguing,' Abby said defensively, but the closeness that had overtaken them since the delivery seemed to have gone, and to her surprise she missed it. 'I was just...' Her voice trailed off and after a reluctant pause she finally spoke. 'I was just moaning...' A smile wobbled on the edge of her lips as Kell waited for her to finish.

'Again.'

'Ready to see the rest of your place?' His smile returned as Abby nodded. 'Bathroom.' Flinging open the door, Kell carried on walking as Abby poked her head in briefly. 'Laundry.' Opening a cupboard, he gave a wicked smile. 'Washing powder. And if I'm not mistaken, there's even an iron. All mod cons here.'

'Very funny,' Abby retorted, following a very broad back along a very narrow corridor.

'Bedroom.'

Suddenly, Kell's voice sounded thick as if he had a cold or had suddenly developed hay fever, but with a notable absence of flowers and not a sneeze in sight Abby could only assume that the sight of the vast queen-size bed was having a similar effect on Kell as it was on her.

A flimsy mosquito net dusted over the bed, the whirring fan billowing the voile gently against the crisp white sheets, emitting a low throbbing hum in the semi-darkened room, and for an inexplicable moment, never had a bed looked more tempting.

'I think we've earned a drink,' Kell said gruffly. 'And if I know Shelly, there'll be a few in the fridge.'

Eternally grateful he wasn't suggesting the pub,

Abby's answer was for once positive. 'Help yourself. I'm going to make my acquaintance with the shower.'

'Better?'

Rubbing her hair with a large towel, Abby stepped into what was supposed to be her lounge and amazingly didn't feel like a total stranger. She hadn't known what to wear, but a pair of too new jeans seemed about right and a black sleeveless T-shirt was surely casual enough.

'Much.'

'I made some supper.' The table had been haphazardly laid, and a slab of cheese surrounded by crackers beckoned her. 'But we could head down to the pub now if you're starving, or there are a couple of steaks in the fridge.'

'This will be fine.'

Better than fine actually. Loading her knife with soft Camembert, Abby scraped it along a cracker before biting in. Never had cheese and crackers tasted so good, and as Kell poured iced water into two glasses Abby rallied at the prospect of more time with him.

'We'll have to go over soon,' Kell added. 'The locals will never forgive me if we don't go and fill them in.'

'What's with the *we*?' Abby questioned, nervous at the prospect of facing everyone, far happier to keep a professional distance. 'It won't take both of us to deliver the news.'

'It took both of us to deliver the baby,' Kell pointed out. 'Don't miss your pats on the back, Abby, it's one of the perks of the job.'

'So, are you always so laid back?' Abby asked, resuming the conversation that had taken place in the warm euphoric glow of the baby's birth.

'Yep,' Kell said simply, before elaborating. 'The only

trouble is that it doesn't last. Me, I worry after the event. Give me a drama and I cope. Honestly, Abby, I don't know why, but you can throw anything at me and I'm like a textbook, I just see what needs to be done and do my best to get on with it, I don't even break a sweat. But afterwards...' Kell let out a breath. 'I'll lie awake tonight imagining every possible thing that could have gone wrong. What if I'd still been waiting for your plane to come in? What if the head hadn't delivered easily? What if—'

'I get the picture,' Abby moaned. 'Unfortunately it hits me there and then. I'm constantly picturing the worst-case scenario.'

'It's just the way you work.' Kell shrugged. 'And it probably makes you a great emergency doctor. Hell, if I'm in trouble I want a doctor worried on my behalf.'

'And I want a nurse who's calm and efficient.'

'Hey, maybe we'll make the perfect team.' Those dark eyes were smiling and that brittle exterior Abby normally so effortlessly portrayed seemed to be crashing down around her as she smiled back at the man beside her.

'Maybe we will,' she said softly. 'Maybe we will.'

Everything about him screamed contradiction.

Everything about him had Abby entranced.

'You don't look like a nurse,' Abby ventured, plunging her knife back into the cheese, flustered by her own rather personal observation.

'You mean I don't look gay?' Kell laughed at her rather shocked features, but Abby quickly recovered.

'Actually, add a handlebar moustache to those boots and skimpy shorts and you'd be a wow at the Sydney Mardi Gras!'

'I was decorating!' Kell laughed. 'Anyway, in case you were wondering, no, I'm not gay.'

It had never even entered Abby's head that he might be. Not for the briefest second. Some men might throw up that question every now and then, and a male midwife, oozing compassion and in tune with a laboring woman, might bring about one of those occasions, but somehow Kell wore it all well. 'I wasn't,' Abby said quickly. 'You just look more like a—'

'Labourer,' Kell suggested, totally unabashed. 'Hell, you're a snob, Abby.'

'No, I'm not,' Abby replied hotly, and then gave him a worried look. 'At least I hope I'm not.'

'Well, I'll choose to reserve judgement on that. And for your information I am a labourer and a drover, too, and a few other things in between.'

'A real Jack of all trades?' Abby said lightly, but her forehead creased slightly. 'What's a drover, by the way?'

'A cowboy to you.'

'Oh.'

'Well, almost a cowboy. And while we're making personal observations about each other, you don't exactly look like an outback doctor.'

'I know,' Abby groaned, then checked herself. It wouldn't do to voice her misgivings to a local, so instead she assumed what she hoped was a more positive tone. 'But I'm really excited to be here.'

It didn't fool him for a second! 'That's not what I heard.' Kell grinned, topping up her glass of iced water then his own. 'I was under the impression you were only here under sufferance.'

'You know?' Abby gulped. 'But if you know, that means…'

'It's OK,' Kell moved quickly to reassure her. 'Ross

only mentioned the fact you didn't really want to come to me, no one else knows. Reece Davies is a friend of Ross's and apparently he was singing your praises when he volunteered you for the job. Ross just told me to treat you a bit gently and make sure that people didn't give you too much of a hard time until you'd found your feet a bit.'

'Honestly,' Abby checked, 'you're not put out that I only came because I had to?'

'That's the reason most doctors come.' Kell shrugged. 'Let's face it—it's a pretty weird place to be. Ross had a passion for it, but he's the exception rather than the rule. The outback's screaming for doctors...'

'So you have to take what you can get?'

'Not at all,' Kell refuted. 'Reece wouldn't have recommended you if he didn't think you were up to it, and Ross wouldn't have taken you on just to have another name on the staff roster. The outback's precarious enough without carrying people. You're here because you're wanted, Abby. The only person who's not happy with the decision is you.'

'Oh, I don't know,' Abby mumbled. 'I've been practising medicine for nearly eight years now and this afternoon is going down on my list of top ten moments. If there's a few more of them around then it's been the right choice. I can see what Reece was saying more clearly now. It's easy to get caught in all the high-tech stuff, but if this is the buzz grass roots medicine gives, then maybe these next three months won't be so bad after all.'

'Maybe not.'

They shared a smile, a tiny smile but it was loaded with hidden meaning. Confused, Abby stood up, and for something to do she grabbed the water jug and headed off to explore her new kitchen, her mind buzzing, every nerve in her body suddenly screaming. A couple of hours in Kell's company and she was acting like a hormone-ravaged teenager, not a sensible thirty-something doctor.

'What's this?' Abby asked, pulling open the fridge.

'I would have thought a lady like you would know champagne when she sees it.'

'I meant, what's it doing in the fridge?' Abby asked, refusing to jump.

'Shelly would have left it there to welcome you. We could always wet the baby's head?'

It could almost have passed as an innocent question, but there was a look in Kell's eyes and such a heavy throb in the air that Abby knew her reserve would pop with as much oomph as the champagne cork, and that was one path she definitely wasn't going to take.

'We'd better get over to the pub. At this rate we won't even make last orders.'

'You're joking, aren't you? The news of the baby will have the pub pumping to the wee hours. It could be a long night.'

'Not for me.' Abby shook her head. 'I'll have a quick orange juice and say hi, and then I'm out of there. I need to be on the ball, and something tells me Ross isn't going to be around very much over the next few days to ease me in.'

'Then it's just as well you've got me.'

Another simple statement, but again Abby felt the throb of sexual tension, the path of a conversation littered with possible innuendo, and she almost took a tentative step, almost responded with a loaded answer herself. But she pulled back in an instant, Kell's easy smile making her wonder if her mind was playing tricks.

'I'll just go and get changed. You do whatever women do before they go out.'

'But where are you going?' Abby asked as he headed for the front door.

'I rent the house next door.' He either ignored or didn't notice the shocked look on her face, carrying on chatting in his usual easy style. 'I only use it for when I'm on call and if I'm on a late then early shift, but I guess it kind of makes us neighbours.'

She didn't answer, Abby truly couldn't, just stood there dumbfounded as he turned and left; the five minutes it took Kell to wash and change nowhere near enough time to get her head together.

Not only was she going to be working alongside him, he would be living next door to her as well.

Three months.

The words didn't console Abby this time.

After only three hours in Kell's company already Abby's nerves were on fire…

CHAPTER THREE

'PUMPING', was a slight exaggeration on Kell's part, Abby decided, but the pub was certainly lively.

Walking in, Abby braced herself for a few curious stares, but the cheer that went up as they both entered almost floored her.

'What's all this for?' Abby gasped as her back was slapped so vigorously that, had she been choking, her airway would undoubtedly have been cleared in two seconds flat. Jugs of beer were being held up in all directions as Kell guided her through to the bar.

'You just delivered Tennengarrah's newest resident, remember?'

Oh, Abby remembered. After all, how could she forget? But never in her wildest dreams had she expected this kind of reception. The births she had witnessed at the hospital had been accompanied with a certain amount of euphoria, a jubilant husband, a few relatives, but the long lonely walk back to the doctors' mess had meant any emotions had been left in the delivery room.

But here! The whole town seemed to be out, cheering and applauding.

'Abby, this is Jack Brown,' Kell introduced. 'Tennengarrah's one and only policeman.'

Another smiling face appeared before her. 'Glad to have you on board, Abby,' Jack grinned, 'playing midwife's not my favourite pastime, you did a great job.'

Another pat on the back, another vote of confidence to make her feel as if she had done something really

44

special. In fact, by the time the obligatory toasts had been made, and her hand shaken by every last person at the bar, Abby found herself starting to agree with them.

It really had been special.

'They'll settle now.' Kell grinned, guiding her to a table. 'A birth's big news here, but when the cricket's starting...'

Abby's eyes followed his to the massive screen in the corner, every head in the place seemed to be turned to it.

'It's all a bit much to take in, I guess.'

Abby took a sip of her juice and gave a small shrug.

'Or perhaps there's not enough to take in?' Kell asked perceptively. 'It must seem a bit of a small world here to you.'

'It's just not what I'm used to,' Abby admitted. 'I'm not saying my way's better than yours or anything, it's just different, that's all.' Taking a breath, Abby decided to deal with a niggle that had been bothering her. 'I'm sorry if I came over as snobby or superior when we first met. It was just nerves, I guess.'

'I was just teasing when I said you were a snob.' Kell was smiling at her. Even though Abby still couldn't look, she could almost feel the warmth of it, almost see the wide dark lips breaking apart in an easy smile.

'I know, and no doubt I'm going to have to get used to it. I'm quite sure there'll be more than a few embarrassing moments. To date I've always lived in the city, always worked in big teaching hospitals, where I just blended in.'

'I doubt that.' The beer glass in his large hand seemed tiny, and Abby found herself staring at it as Kell carried on talking. 'I can't imagine a woman like you ever blending in.'

She chose to ignore that little gem, casting her mind around frantically for something to say. 'Do you ever get fed up?'

Kell shook his head. 'I don't get the time to get fed up.'

'And you've never thought of working in a city?'

Again Kell shook his head. 'I did some of my course units there, but it wasn't where I wanted to be, I was always more than happy to come home.'

'So you've never thought about…' Taking a nervous sip of her drink, even Abby herself could barely believe the personal nature of her question. 'About moving away?'

'Why would I?' Kell shrugged. 'I've got everything I need here. A great job, my family nearby. They run a large cattle station out of town,' he explained, 'so there's never a chance of being bored, and though there are relatively few people here, at least I know most of them. I could never leave this place, Abby. Tennengarrah isn't just a town in the middle of nowhere to me, it's home.'

'So what made you choose to do nursing?' Abby couldn't stop herself. Undoubtedly he was a great nurse, she'd witnessed it for herself today after all, but it just seemed such a strange career choice for a man so in tune with the land, for an *almost* cowboy!

He didn't answer straight away. From the cheers and 'Howzats' flying around the pub, Australia had obviously taken a wicket and Kell stood up to watch the replay as Abby sat there, feigning interest.

'Golden duck,' Kell said, sitting back down with a grin.

'Sorry?'

'You've no idea what I'm talking about, have you?' He grinned as Abby shook her head, then leant forward a touch. 'Mum had cancer.' His voice was still light, but Abby saw the pain behind the frown that flittered across his face. 'Every few weeks we headed off to Adelaide for her chemo. I used to go with her and I guess that's how it started. I'd never even given nursing a thought before, still didn't then really, but later...' Abby watched as his Adam's apple bobbed in his throat, and Kell took a drink before he carried on talking. 'When it became terminal Mum wanted to be at home, and why shouldn't she be? The whole town loved her, wanted to help look after her, be with her...'

'But there wasn't anyone?' Abby ventured.

'Oh, no, we had the clinic. It was tiny then, one doctor and one nurse, Clara. You'll meet her tomorrow, she's great. She made all the difference in the world. Sure, Mum had more friends and neighbours than you could count, all willing to help, but it was Clara who came at two in the morning to up her morphine infusion, Clara who turned her, worked out the meds with the doctor, Clara who made all the difference. I went out on a couple of her clinics, saw the work she was doing and I knew then I'd found what I wanted to do with my life.'

'Did you think of studying medicine?' Even as she asked her question Abby winced, wishing she could take it back.

'No,' Kell said, grinning widely at her embarrassment. 'Because, believe it or not, I'm not a frustrated doctor. I harbour no secret desires to step into your shoes.'

'I'm sorry,' Abby said again. 'That came out wrong. It's just that, as you pointed out, the outback's desperate for doctors...'

'It's desperate for nurses, too, and as much as I love this place, ultimately it's *my* life. I'm not going to be a martyr and do something I don't want to.' Leaning forward further, he beckoned Abby closer. 'Just to clear things up once and for all, I got the grades to do medicine and I chose not to. You're looking at one happy nurse.'

'Glad to hear it.' Her eyes, which had for so long been avoiding his, eventually gave in and met his, and finally she held his gaze, the depth of his stare mirroring the depth of his personality. The multi-layered package she was gleefully peeling back, like a child's game of pass the parcel, frantically ripping off the paper, each layer producing its own small gift, a tiny reward for her efforts.

'Another drink, guys?' Mal, the bartender, broke the moment, flicking a cloth across the table, picking up their glasses.

'Not for me, thanks.' Abby stood up quickly, glad of the intrusion, the chance to catch her breath, to break the heaviness of the aura that surrounded them.

'Nor me.' Kell drained his glass in one gulp. 'I'm on an early shift in the morning.'

Strange the lift that snippet of information gave her.

In contrast to their entrance, their departure went almost unnoticed. A few goodnights, a few cheery waves and they were back to the cricket, leaving Kell and Abby suddenly shy in the warm night air, the ten-minute walk back uncomfortable, and it was a notable relief to finally be at her door.

'Thanks for everything today.' Abby hated the formality of her words, the stilted sound of her voice, but it was the best she could do.

'Hopefully you'll have a gentler start tomorrow.'

'I hope so.'

There was no dead lock to fumble with, no security doors or bolts to pull back, just one push and the door slid open, just one step away from ending the evening. She fumbled for a second in the darkness, trying to locate the light switch.

'Here.' The light that flooded the hallway was a pale comparison to his touch, their fingers meeting on the switch, the embarrassed pull back as a touch that shouldn't matter suddenly did, and the tension that had surrounded them, the distant throb of desire shot into gear, lurching forward a notch as the silence grew louder, the mental music stopping, and Abby knew that the parcel was in her hands now.

The game had ended and peeling back the final layer would reveal the biggest prize of all.

'I've got champagne in the fridge.' Her eyes never left his, testing his reaction, unable to believe her own abandonment.

'I thought you'd never ask.'

The pop of the cork was so loud Abby was sure the whole town must surely have heard it. Giggling in a way she hadn't for so long, she located two mugs, catching the cascade of frothy white bubbles spilling out of the bottle, running rivers along Kell's strong hands.

Passing him a mug, they raised their hands, the pretty china clinking as the mugs met in a toast. 'To...' Abby gave a small laugh '...whatever her name may be, welcome to the world, little lady.'

'And to Dr Abby...'

'Hampton,' Abby filled in.

'To Dr Abby Hampton. That's a nice name actually,' Kell said, as if it really somehow mattered. 'Welcome to Tennengarrah.'

Catching his eyes, a sudden sense of panic engulfed her, an urge to throw back the parcel, to stop this game before it got way, way out of hand, but it was too late for that now. Everything about him was so damned sexy, so mentally, emotionally stimulating, reason barely got a look-in. All Abby knew at this moment was that she wanted him, wanted Kell more than she had ever wanted a man in her life.

She wanted to be the winner, wanted to unwrap her parcel, wanted to taste a moment in his arms, didn't want to go through the rest of her life not knowing how it felt to be held by a man like Kell. Never had she felt such a connection, experienced such an overwhelming mutual attraction, and though the questions, the warning bells alarming in her head were irrefutably warranted, for once Abby chose to ignore them; for the first time in her ordered life, logic lost to passion, desire overrode reason. Surely Kell was a risk worth taking?

He even made denim look sexy.

Until now, jeans had just been that—jeans. Something you pulled on when you couldn't be bothered or didn't have time to think what to wear, a lazy answer almost. But there was nothing lazy about the way Kell wore them, pale and soft against his strong legs, legs that were walking towards her now, taking a step closer, one firm hand taking the mug from her tense hand and placing it carefully on the kitchen bench behind her before bringing his fingers to cup her face, fingers still cold from the champagne, a contrast to the lips so warm, so full, Abby couldn't help but respond, couldn't help but kiss him right back, melt a little closer into his body as she felt his warm smooth tongue slide between her parted lips. And as she slipped from doctor to woman, she knew, as he pulled back slightly, as those black eyes met hers, that she was lost, that the only possible conclusion to this teasing taste was to sign up for the whole package.

No man had ever carried her before, no man had ever

swooped her up in strong arms and taken her to the bedroom, and no man had ever even come close to kindling the passion that overwhelmed Abby.

She had to have him.

It was as basic as that.

Had to have him near her, on her, inside her.

The chore of undressing, the usual clumsiness that broke so many moments didn't even get a look-in. Their T-shirts were discarded in seconds, but every button on his jeans was a pleasure, a slow, unhurried delight, her fingers shaking slightly as she glimpsed the stomach that had teased her only this afternoon, the belly button she had wanted so much to touch. She could now. Her white French manicured nails dragged teasingly around the dark, dark hair as he undid her bra, slipping the lace straps over her shoulders until the cream of her breasts flattened against his chest, the white soft flesh such a contrast to the mahogany of his taut, toned body. Catching her breath, he snaked her own jeans past her hips, brushing her thighs then dusting the scratchy denim over her calves until finally nothing separated them, and as he buried his fingers into her damp, needy warmth Abby groaned in primitive wantonness.

A wantonness that embalmed her, overrode her usual reservations, defied all logic.

Shuddering in his hand, her breath coming in small gasps, she snaked a leg around his thigh, urged him closer. Stretching on tiptoe, she raised herself against his solid manhood, her gasps increasing as he slipped inside. His hands were holding her buttocks now, lowering her down on him, taking her weight with such ease Abby realised then the strength of Kell, that his muscles weren't manufactured in some gym, empty hours pumping iron to earn the perfect body. Instead the grit of hard

work had given him this divine body, and how she rev-
elled in the strength. How divine to feel so light, so
feminine, every fibre of her being on high alert as effortlessly he lowered her back on the bed, their most
intimate parts still entwined as she rested her shoulders
on her bed, and pulled him deeper inside, Kell standing,
pushing, beckoning her on to a place she'd never been,
the peak of her orgasm so intense, such a release, only
then did Abby realise the tension that had held her together, the strain of the past few weeks dissolving as she
shuddered under his touch, as a sob escaped her lips, as
tears she hadn't known were there sprung forth and she
wept with sweet release.

Her tears didn't faze him. Instead he scooped her into
his arms, held her, comforted her and told her over and
over that it was all OK, comforting her like a child,
slipping a cool sheet over them, tucking his body into
her back and stroking her hair, letting her cry those inexplicable tears until finally Abby fell into the deepest,
sweetest sleep.

Oh, no.

Abby didn't say it, but the words resounded over and
over in her mind as gradually the unfamiliar room came
into focus. The overhead fan was still whirring, the sheet
billowing gently in ripples over her body, a lazy hand
holding her closely as Abby lay rigid, her eyes clamped
firmly closed, determined to feign sleep for a few moments until her mind hopefully made sense of the chaos
that she'd awoken to.

How?

The single word was the prelude to a multitude of
questions that stamped through her mind demanding
answers.

How had she let this happen?

How could she have let her guard down like that? She was here to work, to focus on her medical skills, to get her life back on track, not tumble into bed with the first man she met.

But it hadn't been like that, Abby acknowledged. Something much bigger than sex had happened last night. Kell had strolled into her life and into her heart with such breathtaking ease and it would be so easy, so very easy to let him stay.

And that was what scared her the most.

'Morning!' That hand wasn't being so lazy now. Instead, it was working its way along the curve of her hip, moving leisurely along to her stomach, moving relentlessly upwards toward the soft swell of her breasts, and for a second or two, or maybe a moment even, it felt so good, so right, Abby was tempted again to just flow with it, to let the balming effect of his touch soothe her again, to give in to the mastery of Kell's touch.

'Don't.' Her hand gripped his tightly, but there was no need. As soon as the word left her lips, Kell stopped his relentless, sexy exploration and she felt him exhale, and even though Abby's back was to him she sensed the frown on his forehead.

'What's wrong, Abby?'

Scarcely able to believe her ears, Abby wriggled free of Kell's embrace and turned to face him, scooping the sheet around her and trying to cover a determinedly escaping bosom.

It didn't go unnoticed by Kell. She watched his eyes flick downwards, the sheen of early morning lust in his eyes, and again she was assailed with an urge to stop the fight now, to just make love to him and then deal with the consequences.

'What do you think is wrong?' His frown annoyed her now, and Abby sat up smartly, dark tousled hair tumbling down her back, her eyes aghast. 'You, here in my bed, that's what wrong!'

'It didn't feel wrong last night,' Kell said easily. 'In fact, till about two minutes ago it felt pretty damned good to me.'

'I'm not talking about last night,' Abby said, trying to keep her voice even, desperately trying to cast aside the memories of their delicious love-making. She had to put an end to this here and now, to ring the bell and get off at the very next stop, before this journey took her to a place she definitely wasn't prepared to go to. 'I'm talking about now. How I'm supposed to deal with this.' She looked at his incredulous face, visibly shocked at the hysteria in her voice. 'I'm sure you won't believe this but falling into bed with someone I've just met isn't a regular occurrence. In fact…' She took a deep stinging breath, her cheeks flaming as she spoke. 'This has never happened to me before.'

'Nor me.'

Abby gave him a wide-eyed look. 'Oh, sure.'

But Kell didn't seem bothered by the obvious disbelief in her voice, instead he just propped himself up on his elbow and gave his usual easy smile. 'It hasn't,' he insisted. 'Something happened yesterday, Abby, something neither of us was expecting. The second you stepped off that plane there was…' She watched his full mouth struggle to find the words, to articulate something so impossible to define, but, full credit to him, Abby registered, Kell tried. 'There was an attraction, a reaction, whatever you want to call it, but it was nothing you or I had a say in. What happened last night, well, it was special, Abby. Don't ruin it now.'

'Ruin it?' Her voice rose slightly and Abby swallowed hard, raking a hand through her hair, desperately struggling to stay calm. 'Oh, I can tell you about ruining things! I'm an expert! How am I supposed to face everyone? How am I supposed to exert any semblance of authority when I go and have a one-night stand—'

'Hey.' Kell was standing now, his raw nudity causing Abby to flinch. Sensing her embarrassment, he hastily pulled on his discarded boxers as Abby pulled the sheet tighter around her. He didn't look quite so amenable now. If anything, he looked annoyed, those dark eyes narrowing at the edges, deep lines furrowing his brow.

'Firstly, you don't have to worry about how you're going to face everyone because, apart from you and yours truly, no one else is going to know.' He watched her disbelieving shrug and his shoulders tensed. 'They're not. I'm hardly going to go rushing around the town telling everyone. I happen to think that what happens in a bedroom should stay in the bedroom.'

She believed him, albeit reluctantly. As Abby looked up, she knew, as little as she knew him, that Kell wasn't the sort to shame a woman. The blissful time in his arms had taught her that at least. 'What if Ross and Shelly saw…?' Abby said quickly, refusing to be comforted.

'They've got a brand-new baby to deal with. I'm sure they've got better things to be doing than peering out of the window to check whose house I'm going to.'

Abby gave a grudging nod, but Kell hadn't finished yet. 'Secondly, having not had the pleasure of working with you yet, I can't comment on your methods, but I'll tell you this much, Abby, you can exert as much authority as you like out here, but it isn't going to get you very far. We work on mutual respect here. And thirdly…'

Abby took a deep breath and looked up.

'Is this lecture over yet? I'd like to have a shower!'

'And thirdly,' Kell carried on, ignoring her obvious desire to end the conversation, 'you're the one relegating what happened between us to a one-night stand. For what it counts, it meant one helluva lot more to me than that.'

Abby didn't answer—she didn't really get a chance to. In two seconds flat Kell had pulled on his jeans, T-shirt and boots, and without further acknowledgment stomped down the hall. Only when the front door was none too gently closed, and all that was left was the scent of him, did Abby remember to breathe again.

CHAPTER FOUR

'You must be Abby Hampton,' a smiling, friendly, freckled face greeted her as Abby tentatively pushed open the door of the clinic. 'I'm Clara, one of the nurses here.'

That went without saying. Clara was dressed in smart blue culottes, topped with a crisp white and blue blouse emblazoned with various badges, and Abby was somewhat taken aback, immediately regretting her own unusually informal attire. She had expected, what, she wasn't sure, but even in the city rarely were nurses so smartly dressed these days, but Clara looked as if she'd stepped out of a nursing brochure as she let out a gurgle of laughter.

'One of the nurses! That makes it sound like we're spoiled for choice, doesn't it? Apart from me there's Noelene, she's part time, very part time,' Clara added with a slight edge to her voice. 'Then there's Shelly, who I'm sure you've guessed is on maternity leave, and Kell, you've met him already, haven't you?'

That seemingly innocent question had Abby's cheeks flaming and she gave a brief nod.

'He met my plane.'

'And a bit more besides.' Clara was still smiling and Abby thought she might faint on the spot. Surely Kell hadn't told her already! 'I was on yesterday,' Clara said, as if that explained everything. 'And let me tell you, you don't have to worry about proving yourself to the locals, you've already done it. Dealing with a breech delivery ten minutes into your arrival has pretty much sealed your approval rating!' She carried on smiling as Abby let out an audible sigh of relief, scarcely able to believe that the drama of the birth yesterday had been so quickly relegated in her mind.

Kell, or rather her behaviour with Kell, was the only thing on it at the moment.

'Good morning.'

On cue Kell appeared and Abby stiffened at the sound of his voice, turning in what she hoped was a casual manner, but her rather forced greeting died on her lips as she took in the delicious view that greeted her.

Gone was the labourer, the cowboy, the jack of all trades, in his place a smart, very smart, and extremely efficient-looking male nurse. His hair was still damp from his shower but, instead of falling in the chaotic manner of yesterday, it was neatly combed, a touch too much on the collar for the old-school type but smart all the same. A crisp white shirt with dark epaulettes on the shoulders was tucked into a pair of very neat navy shorts, and the Blundstones boots had been replaced with dark brown boat shoes.

Anticipating the laid-back style of the bush, Abby had settled for lilac shorts and a white T-shirt but, looking at Clara and Kell, Abby realised she was woefully underdressed. A bush clinic it may be but the nurses here were serious professionals.

Rather than looking at him, Abby peered at his name badge. Kell Bevan. A rueful smile tickled the edge of her lips as Abby finally dragged her eyes up to meet his.

At least she knew his surname now.

'What's Kell short for?' Abby asked, curious despite herself.

'It isn't short for anything.'

'Well, you two don't need any introductions,' Clara said crisply. 'I'm sure you got to know each other yesterday. Is she very cute, Kell?'

'Oh, very,' Kell said with a devilish grin as the colour swooped at breakneck speed up Abby's neck. 'I'm sure she'll break her fair share of hearts.' And though it was an entirely appropriate response, though Clara carried on smiling as Kell kept talking, Abby would have sworn on anything she could have put her hands on that Kell wasn't talking about the baby.

'Do you think Ross will be in?' Clara asked, oblivious to the undercurrents. 'Bill Nash's daughter just rang and she's bringing him over. He's got chest pain and insists it's just angina even though the sprays aren't working. I offered to go over but Martha wouldn't hear of it. I think she's hoping for a sticky beak at the new baby.'

'She's driving him?' Abby said, alarmed. 'With chest pain? What if he arrests?'

'We've told them over and over to stay put, but they simply won't listen.' Kell gestured to a room. 'But just in case your prediction's right, I'd better show you where things are, or would you rather wait for Ross?'

Her cheeks were burning again as Abby remembered how she'd tossed aside his previous offer to show her around. 'You'll do fine.'

The room Kell led her into had Abby blinking in surprise as she entered it. She had expected a few stainless-steel trolleys, a couple of antiquated monitors perhaps, but the room that greeted her, though smaller, was better equipped than her own emergency department in the city. Advanced monitors lined the walls, along with electronic blood-pressure machines and saturation monitors. In fact, from Abby's brief assessment, it had pretty much everything an emergency room could need.

'Pretty impressive, huh?' Kell said, noting her surprise.

'I'll say.' Fiddling with one of the monitors, Abby shook her head. 'I think I'm going to need a few lessons to fly this thing!'

'You'll be all right,' Kell said assuredly. 'We have to be well equipped,' Kell explained, turning on the monitor and running through the various commands as he spoke. 'It's not like an emergency room in the city where you resuscitate people then send them off to Intensive Care or Coronary Care…' He pushed a red button. 'The ECG tracing will print off at the desk now,' he continued, then carried on talking where he had left off, as Abby took her turn to work the machine. 'We'll have the patient in here until the flying doctors get here. Or patients,' he added. 'If there's a fire or a crash or any number of things, we can end up with several patients at a time. You can start a shift one day and not surface for the next forty-eight hours.'

'But we're just an hour or two away from the nearest base.'

'Assuming they're free to come straight out. And as I said, we can have multiple patients in here, the plane will only take one sicky.'

A dilemma that had first emerged in Abby's mind yesterday was making itself heard, and though the atmosphere between them wasn't exactly relaxed, there was definitely an emerging professional respect, which made Abby the one to ask. 'What if Shelly had needed a Caesarean?'

Kell turned and looked at her and the shrug he gave wasn't dismissive, but loaded with meaning. 'That would have been your call.'

His words reached her, and Abby stilled, reliving yesterday's drama with renewed gratitude for the positive outcome.

'I've never done a Caesarean. How would we have anaesthetised—?'

'We'd have dealt with it.' Kell let out a long ragged breath. 'We've got back-up, amazing back-up, and they can advise us every step of the way. But sometimes tough calls have to be made, and advice is great and all that, but when it's on the other end of a phone or radio, that's all it can be.

'Now, on to Bill.' The smile and slight roll of the eyes told Abby there was a lot of water under the bridge there. 'He had a triple bypass five years ago, and the bottom line is he needs another one. He's been to the city, had all the tests, and unless he has the operation, well, you know the outcome.'

'So why doesn't he have it?'

'He wants to end his days here in Tennengarrah. He's convinced if he has another bypass he won't make it, and frankly with that attitude he's probably right.'

'How old is he?'

'Forty-eight.'

'Forty eight!' Abby gasped. 'But that's no age at all. Surely he should be...'

'Forced?' Kell suggested, and Abby shook her head fiercely.

'Told,' Abby offered. 'He should be told the consequences of his decision.'

'Which he has been. Look, Abby, the angina attacks are getting more and more frequent, invariably he spends a couple of days here and Clara and I get a heap of overtime, but nothing Ross or anyone can say will get him on that plane and into surgery. He knows the risks, knows that he might die bumping along in a four-wheel-drive on the way to the clinic, but that's the way he wants it. Tennengarrah's his home, he doesn't want to leave it. I know you don't understand, Abby, and I can see why, but this place…' A wistful look came over his face and his voice lowered a touch. 'It's in your blood, Abby. For someone like Bill to leave, it would be a tough call.' A hooting car made them both look up. 'Your first patient.'

'Second,' Abby corrected, following him out. 'Don't forget yesterday.'

She could have bitten her tongue off as Kell paused and turned slowly to face her. 'And here I was thinking that was exactly what you wanted me to do.'

One look at Bill Nash was enough to tell Abby that he was in trouble. She could hear the rattle of his chest as she crossed the room! His skin was tinged grey and though sweat was pouring off him, to the touch he was cold and clammy.

'Bill, I'm Abby, Abby Hampton—'

'The new doc,' Kell broke in, slipping an oxygen mask over Bill's face as he attached him to a monitor then tied a tourniquet around his thin wrist to bring up the veins in his hand. 'So you just try and relax, Bill, and let Abby take care of you.'

Bill gave a weak nod, leaning forward on the trolley in a desperate attempt to draw breath into his lungs while Kell established IV access and his daughter filled Abby in on the drugs her father had taken.

'Normally the spray works straight away,' the anxious young woman said, wringing her hands as she eyed her father. 'Or at least after ten minutes or so. He wasn't this bad when I rang—he got worse in the Jeep.'

'Well, he's here now,' Abby said kindly, deliberately not voicing her misgivings as to the wisdom of driving

Bill here. Hopefully there'd be time for that later! As she listened carefully to Bill's chest Abby caught Kell's eye. 'Ten milligrams of morphine, please, and I'd like twenty of Lasix as well.' Even before she had pulled the stethoscope out of her ears an ECG tracing was being pressed into her hands by Clara, and Abby didn't have to look too carefully to see that the recording confirmed her findings. Bill wasn't suffering from angina, he was having a heart attack.

'Bill.' Abby came close to his ear and spoke in calm tones. 'Don't try and answer, I know you're very short of breath, just nod if you understand.'

Bill gave a small nod before Abby continued pushing the drugs through the IV bung Kell had inserted the second Bill had hit the clinic. 'There's a lot of fluid on your chest, which is making it difficult for you to breathe. I'm giving you some Lasix now, it's a strong diuretic and will soon get rid of that fluid and have you more comfortable. I've also given you some morphine, the pain will settle in just a moment or two.'

'I'm having—' Bill started, his words faint, but their meaning clear.

'Don't try and talk, Dad,' his daughter interrupted. 'Just try and do what the doctor says.'

But her words just upset Bill who tore at the mask, trying to make himself heard.

'Am I having—?'

'Yes, Bill.' Abby held his frightened eyes. 'You *are* having a heart attack, but we're dealing with it. You just need to lie back and let us do the worrying.'

Amazingly Bill accepted her words and with some relief Abby watched as he nodded then finally relaxed back onto the pillow as the drugs started to take effect.

'Do you want me to put a catheter in?' Kell asked.

Given the amount of diuretics Abby had given Bill, a catheter was necessary and Abby gave a grateful nod just as Ross Bodey arrived somewhat breathlessly at the clinic.

'Sorry, Abby,' he murmured, leaning over her shoulder Ross looked at the ECG. 'I'm already wondering how on earth we managed without you. How about you, Kell?' he asked as Kell came over.

'It's starting to look that way.' Kell smiled, but the smile on his face didn't quite meet his eyes. 'But first things first. How're Shelly and the baby?'

'Great.' Ross's face literally lit up just at the mention of them. 'Although I thought babies normally slept a lot for the first twenty-four hours. Kate's been singing like a lark all night.'

'Kate.' Abby smiled as the word popped out of her mouth. 'Kate Bodey, that's just gorgeous.'

'Thanks,' Ross said with the grinning enthusiasm of a new father. 'She was supposed to be Catherine, but one hour into it we'd reduced it to Kate, so I think that's what's going to go on the birth certificate! Kell,' Ross added, his voice a touch more serious, 'would you mind popping over before you head off for the clinic? Shelly's having a bit of trouble feeding, and she's never...' he gave a small embarrassed cough as Kell listened, totally unfazed '...breastfed. I've tried to make a few suggestions, but I think it might come better from a midwife. Apparently, Matty wasn't well enough to feed when he was born so he got everything through a tube, but Shelly's determined...'

'No worries,' Kell broke him off in mid-sentence. Did nothing ruffle this guy? Abby mused. 'I'll go and see her soon, but for now could one of you have a word with Martha? Bill's daughter,' Kell explained to Abby. 'She's really worked up and it's not helping Bill.'

Ross nodded but Abby moved first. 'I'll do it.'

'Are you sure?' Ross frowned. 'It's a bit delicate. Bill doesn't want surgery—'

'Kell already explained,' Abby responded. 'I'm more than happy to talk to her.'

More than happy, Abby thought as Kell led them both to a small coffee-room. If Bill didn't want surgery that was his prerogative, but Abby wanted to be sure of her facts next time Bill arrived on death's doorstep at the clinic.

'Is this it?' Abby hadn't even closed the door behind him before Martha dissolved into a flood of tears. 'Is this the end for Dad?'

Pulling up a chair, Abby waited for the initial surge of tears to subside, and even though Abby had never even been in this room before, never set foot in the clinic or met Martha until now, she didn't feel uncomfortable.

Grief, fear, the uncertainty of dealing with the human body, was a scene Abby was all too familiar with.

'Your father's had a heart attack, Martha,' Abby said gently. 'And from his history this isn't the first. Am I right?

With a teary sniff Martha nodded. 'He had two before he had his bypass. Dr Bodey warned us that without another operation this was going to happen.'

'Why won't your father have the surgery?'

'He's convinced he won't survive,' Martha said resignedly. 'We've all tried to persuade him, but he's a stubborn old bull, says if he's going to die he wants it to be here, the same as Mum.'

'When did your mother die?' Abby probed gently.

'Two years ago.'

'And Bill, your father, he's been depressed since then?'

Martha gave a small nod then shook her head. 'We've already been there, with Ross. Dad refuses to accept he's depressed, he won't hear of taking any medication, or talking to anyone. He seems resigned to it, as if he hasn't really got anything to live for.' Martha started crying in earnest now. 'I don't want to lose my father, Doctor, he's only forty-eight. Is it too late if he changes his mind? I mean, would he still have a chance?'

Abby gave a tentative nod of her head, but her voice was guarded. 'He's obviously not well, but I certainly haven't written him off. We could stabilise him and the flying doctors could transfer him to a major hospital, but it has to be his decision, Martha, we can't strap him to the plane.'

Martha gave a weak smile. 'Believe me, I've thought about it. So what now?'

'Well, we'll treat the acute heart attack, and the next forty-eight hours will be critical, but if he survives this event, we'll review his meds again, see if we can help make him a bit more comfortable. The medication we'll give him now will hopefully minimise the damage to his heart from the attack, but what's happened this morning certainly isn't going to help his long-term prognosis.'

'Old fool,' Martha said, but not unkindly. 'Why can't he see how much we all need him, how much we all love him?' Standing, she gave Abby a tired smile. 'Thank you, for being direct I mean. Maybe you can try doing a bit more straight talking with Dad.'

'I intend to,' Abby agreed. 'But when he's a bit better.' Her sympathetic smile faded as Martha closed her eyes, paling as she fumbled for the chair behind her. Reaching out her hands, Abby guided her to the chair behind. 'Hey, are you OK?' Abby asked as Martha took a few deep breaths.

'I'm fine. Too much drama on top of an empty stomach.'

But Abby wasn't convinced. 'Let me take a look at you.'

'No.' Martha's voice was firm. 'I'm honestly fine. Can you tell Dad I'll be along in a minute?'

'Sure,' Abby agreed reluctantly, but an internal voice told her that Bill's stubborn streak was clearly hereditary. 'But if you change your mind, you know where you can find me.'

'How is she?' Kell looked up from the notes he was writing as Abby made her way over.

'Upset, understandably. He really ought to be transferred.'

'I know,' Kell sighed. 'Ross is having another word with him, but it would seem Bill's mind is made up.'

Abby looked over at the thin man, attached to monitors, his face covered by an oxygen mask, shaking his head against the pillow as Ross presumably implored him to think again. Even though Abby knew he was getting the right treatment, she also knew that it was only a short-term solution. Bill needed surgery. As Ross made his way over the news only got worse. 'He wants active treatment for the heart attack, but he's made it very clear that if his heart stops or he stops breathing he doesn't want to be resuscitated,' Ross said grimly.

'Well, I'm not sure Bill's in the right state of mind to be making such decisions,' Abby responded quickly. 'He's scared and in pain and he's also had a hefty dose of morphine. In good faith I can't just stand by and watch if he does arrest.'

Abby watched a quick look pass between the two men

and though she'd probably overstepped some imaginary mark for such a new staff member, Abby truly didn't care!

She wasn't here to make friends and influence people, she was here to practise medicine; and medicine, as always in Abby's usually ordered life, came first last and always.

'From the conversation I had with Martha it appears that Bill's depressed.'

'He is,' Ross agreed, but before he could add to his argument Abby stepped in.

'When Bill's medically stable we'll go over his options again. Until then I think it would be unwise to withhold treatment.' To the uninitiated, Abby's statement didn't sound particularly profound, but from the sudden dive in the atmosphere Abby knew her words had hit the mark.

The new girl she may be, but she was also a well-qualified doctor and for Ross to ignore her opinion could have huge legal ramifications!

'I'm sorry, Ross,' she added. 'I understand you know Bill well, but in all good faith I can't suspend my beliefs just because I'm not in my usual surroundings. Maybe a rather more objective opinion is called for. I'll let you know my findings when I've spoken at length to Bill, but until then if anything happens he's to be fully resuscitated!' And turning on her heel, Abby walked off, not really knowing where she was going but hoping it was in the vague direction of the staffroom.

'I don't want to discuss it,' Abby started as Kell followed her in.

'Neither do I,' Kell said grimly. 'It's mobile clinic day today. Ross thought it might be a good idea if you came along, met a few of the locals.'

'What about Bill?'

'There's an emergency bell that goes directly over to Ross's house and Clara will stay with him.'

Abby gave a hesitant nod. A day with Kell wasn't exactly at the top of her agenda, but maybe it was best to get it over with if they were ever going to establish a normal working relationship.

'I'm just going to check on Shelly,' he said vaguely, with no suggestion that she join him, 'and then we'll head off.'

Of course, there was no such thing as just 'heading off' in the outback. An inordinate amount of time was spent checking the cold-boxes, loading them with medicines and vaccinations, before finally Kell did a quick check on the Jeep itself, ensuring the two-way radio was working and there was plenty of water on board.

'How's Shelly and Kate?' Abby asked, attempting to flick a fly and look calm at the same time, determined not to show Kell she was even remotely bothered at the prospect of spending a morning with him.

'They're going really well. Shelly just wasn't positioning her right and only putting her nipple in, so Kate was having trouble latching on.'

'Oh.'

Well, what else could she say? Here was a guy with all the muscles and brawn of a labourer talking about 'nipples' and 'latching on' and not even breaking a blush. Heavens, even the father, a doctor to boot, had had trouble with the subject. Kell Bevan really was a one-off!

'Do you want to get the sandwiches?' Kell suggested as Abby wilted in the already sweltering heat. 'We won't exactly be inundated with burger bars on the way,' he added, noting Abby's rather reluctant stance. 'And a

Thermos of coffee wouldn't go amiss,' Kell shouted as Abby stomped back into the clinic.

So she was the tea girl now?

Opening the fridge, Abby's heart sank lower, if that was possible.

Where was the prosciutto, pastrami, sun-dried tomatoes and olives?

Where were the bagels and crusty rolls when you fancied one?

Pulling a loaf out of the bread bin, Abby made do with the provisions to hand.

Peanut butter or Vegemite wasn't exactly going to provide a gourmet picnic but, then, what had she expected?

She was an outback doctor for now.

'What are you doing?'

Kell's presence made the tiny kitchen even smaller and it wasn't just because of his imposing height either—the very fresh scent of him, the million or so male hormones flying around the air, coupled with the cringe factor of a night of exhausting passion in his very strong brown arms, made buttering a round of Vegemite sandwiches seem suddenly extremely complicated.

'I'm making lunch,' Abby said through slightly gritted teeth. 'Just as you asked.'

'I asked you to *get* the lunch,' Kell said patiently, as if he were talking to a petulant two-year-old, 'not *make* it. Heavens, where would we be if we treated our doctors like that?'

His sarcasm wasn't wasted, and a blushing Abby followed him out of the clinic kitchen into the staffroom where Kell pulled the lid off an esky.

'Fresh damper, cream cheese, roast beef and home-made chutney. There's a bit of room still—I mean, if you're really partial to Vegemite sandwiches.'

'The roast beef will be fine,' Abby said grudgingly, as Kell took two seconds flat to make a Thermos of coffee.

'Be a shame to waste them, though.' Kell winked, grabbing Abby's rather paltry attempt as they went past and somehow managing to look sexy as he ate and walked towards the car.

She sat in the furnace of the Jeep as Kell loaded the esky into the back with her mouth watering. Only then did she realise that, apart from the cheese and crackers she had shared with Kell last night and the meal on the plane, she'd barely eaten a thing in two days.

'Do you want one?' Kell offered, climbing in beside her and turning on the engine.

After a second's hesitation Abby took the wretched Vegemite sandwich, and as the air-conditioning kicked in and the salt of the Vegemite worked its magic, the butterflies that had been present since she had woken in Kell's arms settled a notch.

'Better?' Kell asked after ten minutes or so of driving.

'Much. How far is it?'

'A couple of hours.' He smiled at Abby's rather pained expression. 'Abby…'

The teasing note had gone from his voice and Abby knew what was coming next.

'If you're going to say, "About last night,"' Abby said, staring out of the window and wishing this conversation could be over, 'then don't.'

'I think a few words might be called for.'

Abby didn't want a few words, didn't want a post-mortem as to what could possibly have possessed her to sleep with him. Actually, she didn't need one. As Kell hauled the Jeep over to the side of the red dusty road, the engine still idling to allow the air-conditioning to work, she met those dark eyes for the first time since last night and there and then she answered her own question.

He was divine.

Seriously so.

'I like you, Abby.'

It seemed such a strange thing to say. Not 'I fancy you, Abby' or 'let's pretend last night never happened' or even 'No one will see us out here if you're up for a repeat', and the simpleness of his statement startled her.

'You don't even know me,' was all Abby managed as she picked at one perfectly manicured little fingernail.

'You don't have to know someone to like them,' Kell said seriously. 'You don't have to know their family history and how many sugars they have in their coffee to know how you feel.' When she didn't answer, didn't even manage a half-smile, he carried on. 'I just like you. I like the way that even though you'd never been on a bike before, you got on, I like the way you weren't too intimidated to ask for your computer, that you chatted away to Shelly about getting her whites whiter when I'm sure there was a million and one things you'd rather have been doing...'

That was rewarded with a very grudging smile and Abby was rewarded tenfold with a slightly wider one back.

'I even like the way you stood up to Ross and me this morning. How you put the patient first. It can't have been easy, and I admire you for it.

'Now, on to last night.'

Mortified, Abby resumed her scrutiny of her nail but Kell was having none of it, capturing her chin with one very large but very gentle hand and turning her to face him. 'Hazarding a guess, I'd say last night was completely out of character. I'd be so bold as to suggest that jumping into bed with a male midwife was pretty uncharted territory for you.'

His hint of humour made the whole scorching conversation almost palatable.

'Jumping into bed with anyone is pretty much uncharted territory,' Abby admitted, scarcely able to believe she was prolonging the agony.

'Flowers, meals, chocolates...' Kell suggested as Abby nodded. 'Movies...'

'I hate going to the movies,' Abby said.

'Of course you do.' Kell grinned. 'The theatre, then?' Again she nodded. 'But I'll settle for a video.'

'And a few kisses, working up to the main event, which would take place somewhere a few months down the track?'

'That just about sums it up,' Abby admitted, flicking her worried brown eyes to his. 'Look, what happened last night simply mustn't happen again.'

'Which relegates it to the one-night stand thing you so obviously abhor,' Kell said with annoying logic.

'P-perhaps, but I'm just not in the m-market for a relationship,' Abby stammered. 'There's just too much going on in my life right now to deal with one, that's why last night should never have happened.'

'Don't say that,' he insisted. 'OK, it was probably too soon, and no doubt if we had our time over we'd have taken things a tad more slowly...' His brow furrowed and he shot her a look that made Abby start as he shook his head. 'I'm sorry, Abby, I've gone over and over it and even with the benefit of hindsight I still wouldn't change a thing. Last night was amazing and wondrous and special so, please, please, don't regret it.'

His words stunned her.

Stunned her.

To hear this six-foot-something would-be cowboy speaking so romantically, for him to somehow have turned her scorching embarrassment around and made everything, if not all right, at least bearable, had Abby dumbstruck.

'I don't regret it.' He watched her blink in surprise at her own admission. 'I know I should, and I guess in some ways I do, but...'

'We were good, weren't we?'

That sexy grin was doing terrible things to Abby now; the butterflies were dancing again, but more in sexual excitement than nervousness.

'Let's start again, huh? Only this time I'm not going to lay a finger on you. Sex is completely off the agenda until we're way past the courting stage. I'll see what I can do on the flowers and chocolate front but the theatre might be a bit of an ask. Still, if there's any local plays on in town I'll be sure to book two of the best seats.'

'You don't have to date me,' Abby said. 'Like I said, a relationship...'

He put his hand up to halt her. 'I'm not going to date you Abby,' Kell corrected her. 'I'm going to woo you, and I'm going to it so damned well that by the time I'm finished with you, a relationship will be exactly what you want!'

She was grateful when Kell ended the conversation and as he flicked the engine back to full life and pulled off the handbrake, Abby realised with a flood of relief that the shame of last night, the utter mortification, had thankfully all been left somewhere on the dusty outskirts of Tennengarrah.

OK, Abby reasoned, last night hadn't been the most sensible thing she had done in her life, but it certainly hadn't been the worst.

In fact, in the scheme of things, Abby mused as the Jeep jolted along the endless red earth, finally accepting the massive Akubra hat Kell offered when the sun was too hot on her dark hair, when she was old and grey and pulling memoires out of a crocheted hat, last night would be right up there, along with her getting her medical degree, her first delivery, her first kiss even.

Stealing a surreptitious look at Kell from under the rim of her hat, a tiny sigh escaped from her lips.

Who was she kidding?

Last night took centre stage.

CHAPTER FIVE

HAD Abby been in any hospital in Australia, in the world come to that, keeping her mind on the job after such a romantic declaration would have been an impossible feat.

But they weren't in a hospital.

Far from it.

In fact, even Abby's earlier vision of a clinic seemed high-tech as Kell swung down from the Jeep and opened the back door.

'We're a bit early, but we'd best get things ready.'

'Where's the clinic?' Abby asked, looking hopefully at the relatively few buildings dotted around the dusty settlement.

'You're sitting in it,' Kell replied cheerfully, opening boxes as Abby tentatively climbed down.

'We work from the back of a Jeep?'

The note of horror in her voice stopped Kell from whatever it was he was doing and he gave her an almost apologetic smile. 'Once every three months the flying doctors come and we get the luxury of working inside their plane, but that happened a couple of weeks ago, so you'll have to wait a while.'

'Considering my contract's only for twelve weeks, I might not even get to meet them,' Abby said, running her eyes along the boxes Kell was opening.

'You're kidding, aren't you? By the time your stint here is up, you'll be on first-name terms with all of them. We do clinics in various parts most days of the week.

There might even be someone here that we need to evacuate today. It doesn't always have to be a high-drama situation to call them out. Nine times out of ten it's an infected wound or unstable asthma, or a complicated pregnancy.'

'What about deliveries?' Abby asked, the drama of yesterday still fresh in her mind. 'Do women in labour come to the clinic?'

'Sort of. I run what could be loosely called an antenatal clinic, and if we anticipate anything other than a straighforward delivery, we'll generally arrange the transfer of the woman to a higher level centre prior to her confinement date. The rest we try to persuade to deliver at the clinic, which can be hard because pregnancy's not really acknowledged in this culture.' Kell grinned at Abby's open-mouthed expression as he carried on explaining. 'But that's becoming less so now. On the whole, the younger people are a lot more open and used to us. You just have to be very wary. What would seem like an obvious remark to make can cause a lot of offence.'

'Such as?' Abby asked. 'I mean, what would you term as an "obvious remark"?'

'When are you due?' Kell responded with a shrug as Abby's mouth dropped another couple of inches. 'Just tread very gently. You'll soon know if you've caused offence because they'll either go all quiet or laugh in embarrassment.'

'So how on earth do you run an antenatal clinic if you can't even acknowledge the fact a woman's pregnant?'

'I've confused you, haven't I?' Kell gave her an apologetic smile. 'Just watch for a while, Abby, you'll soon get the hang of things. As to your question about deliveries, no doubt one afternoon you'll be on your own at the clinic working away and someone will come in in early labour. Now the "normal" thing to do would be to send them away, tell them to come back when they're more advanced, but not so with the local indigenous people. They generally move away from camp when they're labouring and until relatively recently a bush midwife would deal with them.'

'A bush midwife?'

'Unqualified to you, but, believe me, those women have got a lot of experience. Anyway, now we're getting a lot of women come to the clinic, which is great, but again tread warily. If a woman appears in early labour, don't send her home with a cheerful smile and tell her she's got hours to go yet, because if you do you probably won't see her again. Just make her comfortable and probably for the first few times give one of the regulars a buzz.'

'Oh, I'll do that all right!' Abby muttered, shaking her head and feeling more than a touch overwhelmed.

'You'll soon get the hang of it,' Kell said, with far more confidence than Abby felt. 'And here's our very first patient. This will give you a clearer idea, Abby.'

A very thin woman was walking towards them, dressed in a vibrant hot pink dress, carrying a small bundle in her arms.

'Vella,' Kell called as she came closer, his face beaming as he looked at the tiny infant she was carrying. Vella's wary brown eyes looked over at Abby who Kell quickly introduced.

'This is Abby, she's a doctor from Sydney,' he explained, as Vella laid the baby down on the rug in the back of the Jeep.

'When did this happen?' Kell beamed as he gently unwrapped the infant.

'She came too quickly for me to get to you,' Vella said, not answering the question and watching Kell like a hawk as he looked the little girl over.

'She's your fourth, isn't she?' Kell asked. 'Did everything go all right?'

Vella gave a small, embarrassed nod.

'And are *you* feeling OK?'

Again a small nod. 'Just check the baby.'

This was a very new baby, Abby soon realised. The cord was dry but still in place, and she watched quietly as Kell weighed the infant in the old-fashioned hand sling, practically singing encouragement as he swiftly performed a detailed examination of the tiny girl. Checking her spine, her hips for any signs of congenital dislocation, holding her up and then letting her fall into his hand, checking for the startle reflex.

'Wonderful,' Kell said as he measured the infant's head, his fingers probing her fontanelle. Then, like a magician, he pulled out a lolly stick to check inside the tiny mouth.

'She's perfect,' he said, handing the little girl back before broaching the subject of immunisation, to which Vella seemed hesitant. But Kell for the first time pushed a touch.

'Keep Mulla away,' he said. 'In four weeks' time we can give her the first needle, and bring the other children—they should have them, too.'

Vella didn't look too convinced, but at least she wasn't shaking her head now as Kell got out a yellow folder and started to fill it in. Its familiarity touched Abby. The same yellow folder which was given to newborns born in high-tech delivery rooms was used here as well, and she watched as Kell diligently wrote up his findings before handing it to Vella, who with a shy smile stood up then wandered off back into the bush.

'As casual as that visit looked,' Kell said thoughtfully, 'it's been decades in the making.'

He looked at Abby's non-comprehending expression and gave a small smile. 'A case of east meets west, or west meets south.' Still Abby stared at him quizzically. 'The Aboriginal community has its own way of doing things. They have their own system, their own schooling, law enforcement and their own medical beliefs. It's taken a lot of time and patience from both parties for them to accept our ways, or at least some of them.'

He took a swig of water from a bottle then offered it to Abby who without a second's hesitation took it gratefully.

'We can be a bit pompous.'

'So you've told me.'

'I meant the medical profession in general. Sometimes we seem to forget that penicillin's only been around for a relatively short time yet these people have been living, surviving, thriving in the most hostile of conditions since the beginning of time. The Aboriginal people are arguably the oldest surviving race and it hasn't been by chance. As bizarre as it may seem, their ways really do work.'

Abby looked at him thoughtfully. 'Not that well, Kell,' she pointed out. 'The infant mortality rate is appalling. Take what happened with Shelly yesterday—stuck out here, it wouldn't have taken much for it to have been an entirely different scenario.' She wasn't arguing, just pointing out facts, and it felt good.

So surprisingly good to be sitting with their legs dangling out of the back of a dusty Jeep in the seriously middle of nowhere, sharing a bottle of iced water.

'Which is why it's so good that the two cultures are meeting. Sometimes it's hard to hold your tongue, to not insist that things are done your way. You'll see for yourself what I mean soon enough, but for every time you do, you'll be rewarded tenfold. The fact Vella bought her baby to us, that she's probably going to let her have her immunisations and be monitored, is a huge step forward. OK, I didn't get to do a postnatal check on Vella but she's starting to trust me.'

'She is,' Abby agreed thoughtfully. 'Actually, I can remember reading something about—' She didn't get to finish her sentence as Kell dismissed her words with a swish of his hands.

'Don't do that!' he warned with a grin. 'It's OK with me and Ross, but nothing puts the locals more offside than quoting books at them. And I can see their point. Centuries of culture can't really be summed up in a couple of books, so if you're not sure about something, just ask them. They're only too happy to share if you go about it the right way.'

'Is that a gentle warning?' Abby asked, but Kell didn't answer. 'Are you worried that my acid tongue might wither years of diplomatic relations?'

A smile twitched on the edge of his lips and Abby held her hand out for the drink bottle. 'Well, don't be,' she whispered needlessly, standing up as a few people approached the Jeep, looking at her with wary brown eyes, nudging and giggling each other as Abby forced a nervous smile. 'I'm only mean to my colleagues.

'And, by the way what's Mulla?'

'Evil spirit,' Kell whispered. 'And your best line of defence. Believe me, after three months in this place you'll be glad of that word!'

She should have felt supernumerary, should have felt

supremely nervous, watching an efficient Kell effortlessly chat with all the patients, giving needles, pulling
off dressings, checking ears and eyes and handing out
little tubes and bottles.

But she didn't.

Instead, after a couple of nervous starts Abby found
herself joining in. Filling the little yellow child care
books in, with her gold-gel penned scrawl, weighing
cute babies with the hand sling, checking breasts, pre-
scribing antibiotics, even laughing along with the locals
at her appalling attempts at their language.

The sun was hot on her arms and on the back of her
legs, her olive skin no match for the scorching heat of
the early afternoon sun, and when Kell filled her hat with
water then plonked it back on her head, instead of
screeching in horror she sighed with relief as the icy
rivers of water ran down her neck and back and for five
minutes or so Abby remembered what it was like to be
cool as she carried on with the work.

'Can I borrow you, Abby?'

Patting a little girl on the head, Abby smiled at her
mother and made her way back to the Jeep, where Kell
was staring at a nasty-looking wound on a young man's
leg.

'This is Mike, the local mujee, or medicine man. He's
brought Jim to see us—reluctantly,' Kell added under
his breath. 'Jim didn't want to come. What do you make
of this?'

Nodding to Jim, Abby took a closer look at the leg.
It was red and swollen and angry-looking, the area
around the infection blistering with the tell-tale appear-
ance of cellulitis. 'Is it a bite?'

Kell shook his head. 'He thinks he knocked it on a
tree, but never really gave it a thought till it swelled up.'

Abby's mind flicked to the city, to the plan of action she would take there. Order an X-ray, perhaps a small probe in the emergency theatre and some wound swabs, then up to the ward for elevation and IV antibiotics. Kell was obviously thinking along the same lines.

'We could evacuate him.'

'No.' The young man pulled his leg back and with elaborate gestures and a lot of broken English got the message across that his wife was due to have a baby any day now and there was no way he was going in the big plane in the sky.

'You could both go,' Kell suggested gently. 'Lara could have the baby in hospital.'

'No.' Clearly agitated now, he made to go, but Abby put a firm hand on Jim's shoulder.

'Steady, Jim,' Abby said firmly but gently. 'No one's going to make you go anywhere, but I really do need to take a proper look at it.'

Reluctantly he put his leg back down and Abby rummaged through the large metal boxes Kell had dragged onto the floor. 'I thought I saw some magnifying glasses.'

'Here,' Kell pulled them out. 'Do you want an incision pack?'

Abby gave a small nod. It was a tiny procedure, one she did practically every day, but back in Sydney she was in a sterile theatre, and the back of a Jeep didn't even compare, but the thought of Jim heading back into the bush with that nasty infection didn't exactly leave her with a choice.

For a makeshift theatre the Jeep actually sufficed quite well. Hand-washing from a water flask didn't exactly seem sufficient, but with a good rub with alcohol and sterile gloves with about ten times the amount of

Betadine she normally would use, Abby felt confident the wound was prepped enough to explore. Gently she administered some local anaesthetic, and even a very stoic Jim let out a murmur of pain despite Abby's best attempts.

'Mulla,' he moaned, holding his thigh and glancing down every now and then.

'No Mulla,' Abby said cheerfully, as the three men present turned to her with slightly startled expressions. 'I think the problem's a bit more simple than that!' Abby's smile was one of satisfaction as her scalpel hit a hard object. The fact there was something embedded in the wound made the prospect of a satisfactory resolution all the more tangible. 'There it is!' she added triumphantly, working a small dark dot out with her forceps until a large jagged-looking thorn was being held up for all to see.

'Steady, mate,' Kell said as a not so stoic Jim lay back on the floor of the Jeep, beads of sweat on his brow. 'The worst is over now.'

'Not quite.' Abby winced on Jim's behalf. 'I just want to get some of the pu—'

'We get the idea,' Kell interrupted with a wink as Abby took the hint and worked on quietly, taking a swab and then irrigating the wound for ages till she was quite sure the job she had done was anything other than makeshift. Quietly pleased with her work, Abby was just about to put a large sterile dressing in place when Mike tapped her on the shoulder.

'Won't be long now,' Abby said in her crisp efficient tone, even flashing a smile as she looked up briefly.

The smile didn't last long.

With something approaching horror she watched as Mike pulled what looked like an old chamois out of his shorts pocket and with hands a world away from Abby's latexed ones smeared a thick oily goo over the painstakingly cleaned wound then nodded for Abby to continue.

She didn't dare look at Kell, didn't dare look at anyone. Instead, Abby gave a small tight nod and, swallowing hard, resisted the urge to pick up her saline swabs and clean the revolting mixture away. Instead, she placed the wad of combine in place and secured it with a large clear waterproof dressing.

'I'd like to give Jim an injection of penicillin, please, Kell.' She looked at his deadpan face but she could see the flash of a smile in his eyes as he solemnly nodded.

'Sure, Doctor.'

'It should be fine now,' Abby said as Kell helped Jim down. 'But if the redness gets worse or if the pain increases...'

'We will come and see Dr Bodey.'

'Or even me,' Abby added pointedly, and even Mike laughed.

'Or you, yes, Doctor, we will come and see you.'

Watching as Jim limped off, Abby heard a gurgle of laughter coming from Kell.

'You were fantastic!' he enthused. 'Absolutely fantastic.'

'I was just doing my job.' Abby shrugged but her pink cheeks told Kell she was pleased. 'Do you think I pushed it too hard at the end when I said he could come and see me?'

'Mike laughed, didn't he? I tell you, Abby, you're in.' For a second he looked at her, only for a second, but enough time for Abby's cheeks to change from a cute pink to a rather unflattering shade of puce. 'I'm sorry about earlier, I should never have tried to lecture you.'

'Hey.' Abby put her hands up. 'I'll take all the advice

I can get out here.' Her eyes strayed to the one box that hadn't been opened—the esky—and Kell followed her gaze.

'Ready for lunch.'

'I was about two hours ago,' Abby admitted, licking her lips as Kell pulled the esky down. Taking a rug, Abby fashioned a picnic area and poured two mugs of coffee as Kell played a very good mum, pulling off foil and handing her thick wedges of the best bread Abby had tasted, filled with the thickest slabs of beef and cold fried onions, the home-made chutney adding a delicious tang as Abby chewed in what undoubtedly wasn't the most feminine fashion.

'This is divine,' Abby groaned in pleasure.

'Wait till you taste the vanilla slices.'

'I'm going to go back to Sydney the size of a house at this rate. How often do you do the mobile clinic?'

'Most weekdays,' Kell said, ladling more chutney into one of his rolls and somehow flicking the flies away as he did so. 'This is just one of many. Some take a full morning to get to. Still, at least June packs us a bigger lunch so there are compensations.'

'I'll say. So how on earth did Ross manage?'

'He didn't is the simple answer. There was another doctor, Richard Hoskins, but he'd been trying to retire for the past decade. He only stayed on because he couldn't bear the thought of what would happen otherwise. It's good Ross found us or the clinic would have had to close.'

'What would you have done?'

Kell shrugged. 'There would still have been more than enough work, there are a lot of nurse practitioners in the outback, but having a doctor and a well-stocked clinic just makes it all the more interesting. Shelly's a midwife as well, so we're a level-I centre, which means we can have uncomplicated labours. Now, if we could just persuade an anaesthetist to come on board...'

'Oh, so I'm not good enough?'

'You'll do.' Kell smiled. 'You did really well.'

'I did not,' Abby insisted. 'There was nothing done today that wouldn't have been done without me.'

'That's not true.' Kell shook his head so definitely Abby actually found herself starting to believe him. 'That leg was nasty. I was pretty sure it was just straight cellulitis. I was erring on the side of evacuating him, you've saved a call-out.'

'Hopefully,' Abby said thoughtfully, 'now that the foreign body's out, there's a good chance it will heal nicely.'

'And,' Kell said, the laughter evident in his voice, 'you managed not to scream in horror when Mike put his home brew on your nice irrigated wound.'

'Oh, the scream was there,' Abby said grimly. 'What was that stuff?'

'Billygoat weed, and the most amazing thing of all is it works.'

'I'm sure it does,' Abby said, as Kell gave her a slightly startled look.' I don't have a completely closed mind, you know. In the city they're putting honey on wounds now and it's proving more effective in some cases than the most sophisticated antibiotics and dressings, and only last week the vascular surgeons put leeches on some poor girl's finger after microsurgery, and the most amazing part of all is they've probably saved her from having it amputated. There's a lot to be said for alternative medicine.'

'You're a bit of a dark horse, aren't you, Abby?'

'What's that supposed to mean?' He was looking her

in *that* way again, his eyes boring into her, making her blush with the simplest of sentences.

'You come across so brusque, so efficient, so old school, and I don't mind admitting when you stepped off that plane I thought you were about to turn tail and run.'

'I nearly did,' Abby admitted, hiding under the brim of her hat, anything other than meet his eyes.

'And yet here you are now getting down and dirty, mixing with the locals as if you've always been here.'

Abby managed a half-look at him as she bit into her sandwich, but she nearly choked when Kell spoke next.

'What happened, Abby? How come you took up the position when you didn't want to?'

'I told you, if I wanted the consultant's position—'

'That's the formal version,' Kell interrupted. 'Come on, Abby, what's your story?'

Her sandwich was finished so that diversion wasn't open. Reaching for her mug, Abby realised her coffee was down to the dregs. For an age she didn't answer, just stared out at the red dusty view, watching a small wind storm flicking up a few dry leaves and circling them around, little mini-whirlwinds dancing on the plain, and it was only then she turned her troubled eyes back to Kell.

'Why does there have to be another version?'

'Because for all your confidence, for all your brittleness and take-me-or-leave-me attitude, I can't help but think you're a woman with a lot on her mind.'

'You assume one helluva lot,' Abby flared. 'considering we've only just met.'

He didn't say anything, he didn't have to. The truth was, and they both knew it, Kell had in one night got closer to Abby than anyone had in a long time, and the tears she had cried after they had made love hadn't been post-coital bliss, just the sheer overwhelming release of tension.

Her mind flicked back as Abby remembered how he had held her, how good it had felt, how a relative stranger had somehow known how to hold her, what to say.

What not to say.

'Who hurt you, Abby?'

She gave a very short, very false smile, then relented with a shrug. 'No one. I took care of that part all by myself.' When her cryptic words brought no comment Abby carried on talking, her eyes following the dancing leaves, pausing every now and then as the wind dropped, taking the time to regroup, to tell her story as best she could. 'I was going out with another doctor, David. He was junior, one of the residents. When I say going out, it was hardly…' She paused for a moment then cleared her throat. 'We went out for six months. He liked parties, I liked restaurants, he liked pubs, I liked dinner parties.'

'Not the ideal match,' Kell ventured, but Abby shook her head.

'He made me laugh and it felt surprisingly good. I've spent most of my life buried in books, working my way towards being a consultant, it's always been my dream…' Realising she was getting off the track, Abby cleared her throat. 'You know what it's like, there's always some social event you're expected to go to.' She laughed as Kell shook his head. 'Well, there is in the city. Anyway, we went to all the social dos together. I didn't mind when he wandered off with his crowd it was just nice to have someone to go with. Like I say, it wasn't a deep and meaningful relationship.' A blush darkened her cheeks. 'You may find this hard to believe after my behaviour last night but we never even slept together.' She waited for a chortle of laughter, a scoff of disbelief, but it never came. It was as if Kell knew how hard this was for Abby, and he just nodded gently. 'Of course, the rest of the hospital thought we were serious, they didn't realise how casual the whole thing was.

'He was in a car crash.'

Despite the intense heat, Abby shivered, visibly paling as Kell watched her. Placing his sandwich down on the rug, he moved across to where she sat alone, putting his arm around her instinctively, knowing there was worse to come.

'Were you on duty?'

'Oh, I was on duty all right and I tried so hard to save him, but I didn't.'

'You couldn't,' Kell suggested, but Abby shook her head and for the third time in their short history he was witness to her tears. Only these weren't tears of elation after a birth or the release of tension after love-making, these were choked, agonising rasps that seemed to convulse her. He sensed her agony, yet he knew she had to go on, knew that in this case out was definitely better than in.

'I didn't,' she sobbed. 'Because I thought I knew him, because I treated him like a friend, not a patient.'

Kell looked at her, his eyes full of questions, and he screwed them closed when Abby spoke again, feeling her pain as he imagined the scene.

'I didn't order a drug tox screen.'

He let her cry for a moment, held her close till the tears abated slightly and she could talk again.

'He had massive head injuries and internal injuries, but I still think that had I known he was on drugs, if I'd only given him Narcan and reversed the opiates, he might have stood a chance, might have lived.'

'What did the coroner say?' Kell's voice was practical, calm and to the point, and Abby took a deep breath.

'That he died from his injuries, that nothing could have been done.' As Kell opened his mouth Abby shook her head. 'I got a rap on the knuckles, I didn't get off completely scot-free. He pointed out the absence of the drug screen, how lucky I was that it ultimately didn't contribute to his death.' Her voice strangled in her throat as she continued. 'Everyone blames me.'

'I'm sure they don't.'

'But they do. I've heard a couple of the nurses talking and you've no idea how many times I walk into a room and the conversation stops, or they suddenly start discussing the appalling hospital coffee.'

'Hospital coffee is appalling,' Kell said. 'I'm sure it's a frequent topic of conversation.'

'I'm not imagining it, Kell.'

'Maybe not, but have you ever considered they're not talking about your part in it? The fact a doctor was on drugs, came into the department and died, well, that's enough to keep most staff rooms going for months.'

'Maybe,' Abby said tentatively. She had never really thought of it like that and she chewed on her bottom lip, barely noticing Kell's arms were still around her. 'Anyway, whether they blame me or not, it's really immaterial. The simple fact is that I blame myself. I should have treated him as just another patient, not assumed that just because I knew him…' Her bottom lip wobbled and a tear slid down her cheek. 'Or thought I knew him.'

'That must be hard as well.'

Abby nodded. 'There are a million questions buzzing in my head that I'm never going to have the answers to.

Why would someone so young, with everything going for them, who knew all the risks…how could he do it to himself, and if he did have problems why couldn't he have spoken to me?'

'Nobody has those sorts of answers, Abby. People mess up their lives for different reasons and, as hard as it is to watch, sometimes there's nothing you can do to help.'

'I don't believe that.' Abby shook her head firmly, wiping angrily at her tears with the back of her hand. 'There's *always* something that can be done. When I get back to Sydney I'm implementing a new system for the addicts that come through the department. At the moment all we do is treat their symptoms and, depending who's on at the time, perhaps make a referral to the drug clinic or hand them a pile of brochures. I want us to have a more structured approach, possibly some trained counsellors on staff. There's a rapid detox clinic within the hospital, so the basics are in place. We just need to utilise the initial contact in Emergency more effectively.'

'Sounds interesting,' Kell said thoughtfully, but Abby hadn't finished yet. 'And I'm trying to arrange a drug awareness course for the staff, not just to alert them what to look for in patients, but in each other—'

'Abby,' Kell broke in, his voice calm and strong, 'it sounds like you're taking a hell of a lot on.'

'Maybe.' Abby shrugged. 'But someone has to do it. Wringing our hands and saying it's just too big isn't going to help.' Her voice softened and Kell had to strain to catch what she was saying. 'I made a promise.'

'To David?'

Her eyes were glistening with a fresh batch of tears as she nodded. 'After he died, I promised him that I wouldn't let his death be in vain.'

'Do you really think you can make a difference?' His questions wasn't derogatory. Instead, there was a note of admiration, of wonder in his voice as Abby gave a determined nod.

'Absolutely.' She gave a wry laugh. 'That is if Reece ever gives me the consultant's position! There's a bit of spadework that needs to be done there. Apparently, since the night David came in, I'm suddenly the queen of investigations.'

Kell's arm tightened a fraction around her shoulders in a friendly sort of squeeze. 'Running too many tests, huh?'

Abby nodded.

'Total body scan for a fractured toe?'

Again she nodded but there was a tiny smile on her lips.

'Full cardiac work-up for a touch of indigestion?'

Her smile was a bit wider now. 'All the time.'

'And I bet every ninety-year-old who clips the kerb with his car gets a full drug screen.'

She managed a laugh but it was laced with tears. 'Every single one. Reece said that I needed to get back to basics, to practise some grass roots medicine without the luxury of a million radiographers and pathologists.'

'Boost your confidence a bit?' Kell ventured.

'Or shatter it altogether.'

'Oh, I don't think so,' Kell said with a sureness that was alien to Abby. 'A breech delivery unaided, a mobile clinic in the middle of nowhere without even one call to the flying doctors—I'd say that's a pretty good start.'

'I can call them?' Abby looked up sharply.

'With the radio in the Jeep.' Kell grinned.

'But I thought that was just for emergencies, or to get in touch with the clinic.'

'Oh, no, nine times out of ten I radio through at least once each clinic to ask advice from one of the doctors. They'll be wondering where I've got to today. I shouldn't have told you that—you'll be on all the time now.'

'No, I won't.' Standing up, she looked at the ants marching purposefully towards Kell's discarded sandwich. 'You're looking at the new, confident Abby Hampton.'

Kell grinned. 'How about I clean up here and we eat the vanilla slices in the back of the Jeep?'

Never had a change of subject been more gratefully received!

Though she'd dug her heels in, though she'd thought she might die without her laptop and an internet connection, that night, when Abby finally set up the computer and took an age to establish a connection, when she finally hit the 'new mail' button, when she tried to describe the past twenty-four hours of her life, the paltry four-line greeting she sent to her family didn't even begin to encompass the roller-coaster of emotion she had set foot on.

Looking out of the massive glass door, the setting sun illuminating the sky a fiery red, silhouetting one single lonely tree in the endless glowing landscape, Abby truly understood the beauty of the vast outback, took solace in the tiny speck she was in the scheme of things and finally managed to look back on the previous night without her heart skittering into shameful palpitations.

CHAPTER SIX

For all Kell's promise of wooing her, from the lack of attention he paid her in the ensuing weeks, he had obviously thought better of it!

Not a single flower, chocolate or even so much as a video graced Abby's palm or even merited a mention.

Sure, they worked well together, laughed at each other's jokes and rowed about the patients every now and then and, sure, the air crackled with sexual tension like a balloon rubbed on nylon whenever the two of them were together, but whatever game Kell was playing, a quick chase clearly wasn't on his agenda.

Not even a slow one, come to that.

As the days turned into weeks, a gnawing feeling pitted at Abby's stomach, a sense of time moving on, quickly running out, but curiously coupled with a sense of sheer relief.

What was the point of a romance that couldn't possibly go anywhere?

The outback was in Kell's blood, he'd told her that on their first night.

The city pumped in Abby's veins.

Not that she didn't love Tennengarrah, not that the people weren't wonderful, the work amazing and the scenery literally breathtaking, but it wasn't, neither would it ever be, home.

Maybe Kell was right to hold back, Abby mused late one afternoon while, sitting at her desk exhausted after another mobile clinic, yet reluctant to go home. If one night together could feature so heavily in the jigsaw of her life, imagine three months' worth?

Imagine falling in love, and it would be so easy to do, Abby conceded, only to have to kiss him goodbye.

'Right, I'm done.' Snapping the lid on her gel pen, Abby gave a smile to Kell as she walked past.

'See you, Abby,' Kell called cheerfully, hardly bothering to even look up from what he was doing. And though she knew it was for the best, that there was absolutely no point in pursuing this, she couldn't just leave things there.

'Are you on in the morning?' Abby asked, lingering too long at the door.

'Nope.' Kell smiled. 'I've got four days off now. Not that there's going to be much R and R taking place—there's a pile of jobs waiting for me back home.'

Home.

From the little she knew of him, the house he rented next to hers wasn't Kell's home.

Apparently his real home was a massive sprawling property with a zillion cows and an endless demand on his time.

'Oh, well, enjoy.' Abby smiled though her heart sank. She was officially off at the weekend which meant she wouldn't see Kell till Monday, not that he seemed remotely bothered. 'I'll see you after the weekend, then.'

Kell barely looked up. 'Sure. Catch you later.'

Leaving the clinic, Abby bristled with indignation.

Catch you later.

What was she, one of his blessed cows or something?

The evening stretched on endlessly before her. Checking her emails, Abby listlessly read about parties she hadn't been to, the plays she hadn't seen and the new menus she hadn't sampled.

Heavens, it was hot!

Stripping down to her undies, Abby pulled the ring on a can of beer and rolled her eyes, thinking of the fifty-dollar bottles of wine her colleagues were undoubtedly ordering at this very moment.

'It's Monday, Abby,' she corrected herself. Even her favourite restaurant at Darling Harbour would be quiet.

Even the news was different here—in-depth reports on the drought, the cattle markets, the weather gone into in such detail, when in truth it could have been summed up in one word.

'Hot.'

Or two.

'Stinking hot.'

The T.V. commercials might just as well have been in Japanese, the latest breakthroughs in the eternal problem of female exfoliation barely got a mention when there were worming tablets to be discussed or the latest in water tanks to be sold!

She couldn't even break her diet and ring for a pizza, and sitting in the local watering hole with the locals endlessly talking about Tennengarrah's annual ball preparations wasn't really an option in Abby's current restless mood.

What was the point of a ball when Prince Charming so clearly wasn't interested? When Prince Charming had already fitted the slipper and no doubt moved onto pastures new!

'Hey.'

Prince Charming standing with a rather wilted bunch of flowers and a rapidly melting bar of chocolate was the last thing Abby was expecting. And though her underwear was fabulously expensive and undoubtedly flattering, it wasn't exactly the look she was hoping to achieve when Kell finally deigned to drop by.

'Doesn't anyone knock here?' Abby asked, grabbing a throw and tucking it around herself.

'No.' Kell shrugged, but from the way he couldn't quite meet her eyes Abby was sure he wasn't as cool as he looked.

'What are these for?' she asked rather ungraciously as Kell handed her the flowers.

'You said you liked flowers and chocolates, and there's no movie theatre for a few hundred k's, but I've got a good video lined up.'

She actually laughed. 'Four weeks after the event is stretching it, Kell, even allowing for disconnected phones and a family death.' She looked at his non-comprehending face. 'That's the sort of excuses we women come up with when men don't call. Not that you needed to call, Kell,' Abby rambled on. 'We see each other every day at work.'

'I've been trying to play it cool.'

'Well, you've done an amazing job.'

'I figured that if I laid low long enough, you'd realise what you're missing.'

It had worked!

'Are you doing anything?' Kell pressed. 'Tonight, I mean?'

'Actually, I've got a table booked for eight and there's some clothes I need to pick up from the dry-cleaners before they close, but apart from that...' She looked at his blank face. 'Tell me, Kell, what plans could I possibly have in this backwater?'

Her words were too harsh, too condescending, and Abby regretted them, but Kell turning up like this was the last thing she'd been expecting, and letting him glimpse the effect he was having on her was way too dangerous.

It was easier to play it tough.

'Get dressed,' Kell said, ignoring her sarcasm. 'There's something I want to show you.'

Void of a single witty answer for once, Abby didn't backchat him.

For once she did as she was told.

Now they'd slept together, now they'd shared a bed, riding on the back of Kell's bike wasn't such a balancing act!

OK, she had no official claim on him, but their rather too distant shared intimacy at least mentally permitted Abby to hold onto Kell's waist as they belted along the dirt roads, the wind whipping the words out of her mouth as she occasionally spoke. With Kell's back now morally accessible to rest her cheek on, Abby finally permitted herself to relax.

Sort of.

The late sun was still hot on her bare thighs, the engine purring between her legs as they tore through the endless distance, the occasional silver windmill glittering by a thirsty dam.

Tennengarrah *was* beautiful, Abby admitted almost reluctantly, for she didn't want to be enamoured of the land. Didn't want to fall in love with its undeniable charms because surely that could only make leaving harder.

She wanted it to be a job, as bland as a concrete building, a line on her résumé, a means to an end.

Not a life-changing experience.

But it entranced her. It had a rugged naked charm not

unlike Kell and even that analogy seemed fitting, for the land he was so much a part of was so much a part of him.

But the analogy didn't end there.

She didn't want to love Kell either.

Didn't want to admit that the overwhelming attraction that had propelled them to bed was so much more than skin deep. Didn't want to acknowledge that his smile, his walk, every damn thing about him had her in the palm of his hand.

Love was out of bounds.

Love made you do stupid things, like chuck in eight years of hard work on top of six years of study, made you give up long-held dreams of being an emergency consultant, hold back on a promise you'd made to a friend, made you contemplate a life with a dark-haired charmer and a cattle ball once a year and endless dark-haired, dark-eyed, eternally laid-back children.

She simply mustn't go there.

They rode for ever, up winding rocky paths, over bumpy terrain, the bike allowing them access to places even the Jeep couldn't negotiate. She had no idea where they were going and in truth Abby didn't care. Being with Kell such an unexpected treat, the whys and where-fores could wait a while.

Up they went, the landscape more awe-inspiring by the moment, each blink like the shutter of a camera, revealing a more amazing view, and Abby rued that she hadn't even thought to bring her camera. When they finally stopped Kell switched off the engine, pulling off his helmet and shaking his hair, and Abby did the same.

'We'll have to walk the last bit. Are you up to it?'

His question made her laugh. She wasn't quite that feeble!

'Oh, I think I can manage it.'

But a gentle bush walk wasn't what Kell had in mind.

Pulling a backpack on, he led the way, holding her wrist every now and then as she negotiated a rock, or climbed a none-too-small cliff face until finally she knew they'd reached their journey's end, for nowhere on earth could be more idyllic.

Amidst the dry, unforgiving land she surveyed a true oasis. Two massive billabongs carved into the dark red rock, the water as blue and clear as crystal, beckoning her hot, aching body.

'It's beautiful,' Abby gasped, drinking in the view, her eyes finally resting on Kell who gazed at the scene before him with knowing eyes.

'I know.'

'Does it get busy, I mean with tourists…?'

Kell's eyes found hers. 'I've never seen another soul here.'

'Never?' She ran a nervous tongue over her dry lips.

'Never,' Kell affirmed.

'Any crocodiles?'

'None.'

'You're sure.'

'Positive. Do you reckon we've earned a swim?'

Abby wasted no time with false modestly. To have made a token protest, to have forced a blush or pulled a face would have been pointless. After all, they'd more than seen each other naked and perhaps more to the point, after a long hot dusty bike ride never had water looked more inviting!

As they stripped down, as they ran whooping into the icy water, it wasn't even sexual excitement that made Abby feel suddenly alive, though the sight of Kell naked certainly took care of that. No, it was more the thrill of the child within her, the utter joy of being here, and they duck-dived and swam and splashed and grabbed each other's ankles. Abby found that she wasn't such a bad swimmer after all, nowhere near Kell's standard, of course, but, Abby reasoned, if this was his back-yard pool then he had every reason to practise.

'Come on.' Shivering, her fingers and toes wrinkled, her teeth chattering, Abby dried herself with the small towel Kell offered, then waited as he pulled a rug from his bike box and laid it on the ground.

'I've never brought anyone here before.' Abby was about to laugh, to make some light-hearted comment, but she heard the serious note in Kell's voice and knew it would be out of place.

'No one?' Abby checked.

'No one,' Kell confirmed. 'I've always kept it as my own, somewhere to escape to, somewhere to come and think.' He rolled onto his back, and stared up at the darkening sky.

'What are you thinking now?'

'How nice it is to be here with you…'

Abby lay on her back, smiling into the dusk at the quiet lull of his voice, but her smile faded as Kell carried on talking.

'How I don't want you to go.'

She felt his face jerk towards hers and she lay there rigid, staring unblinkingly at the sky filling with stars. And even though what Kell had said was exactly what Abby had wanted to hear, she wished somehow he could take it back, flick the switch and carry on the game they had been playing, that they were friends, lovers once but really just friends. Not this horrible grown-up version with feelings and beginnings and the inevitable end.

'You've ignored me for the last month.'

'I have not.'

'Oh, you've been lovely to me at work, but—'

'Abby, do you not think I've wanted to see you, not wanted to take you out?'

'Then why didn't you?'

Kell gave a low laugh. 'Because I knew the minute I got you alone I'd be moaning how I don't want you to go, getting heavy, doing all the things I've never done before.'

'Never?'

'Never.'

His honesty scared her, the whole thing scared Abby actually, how one man could have her acting so completely out of character, how one night could have the potential to turn her life around so completely and so irreparably she couldn't even begin to contemplate it. And from the serious look on Kell's face he understood the impossibility of it, too.

'It could never work Kell.' She heard him exhale, saw his eyes close, the tiny shake of his head. 'It couldn't, Kell, and you know that as much as I do. We're just too different.' She let out a low laugh, trying to lighten the suddenly dark, volatile mood. 'Can you imagine me getting excited like Shelly is about the annual Tennengarrah ball? Can you imagine me discussing cattle per hectare and the local craft market with Clara?'

Her voice dropped a shade and she tried to keep the tremor out of it as she continued. 'Can you imagine you in the city, Kell, cooped up in some tiny apartment, catching the train or bus to work when you're used to all this?' He didn't answer and his silence tore through her. 'It could never work,' Abby said more lightly than she felt, the reality of her words delivering an agony she couldn't portray to him.

'I'm not a hick, Abby, I wouldn't be like Crocodile Dundee.'

'I know you wouldn't, but it would be a huge move and the truth is I wouldn't exactly be around to make things run smoothly for you. With this drug programme and everything, I'm going to be putting in obscene hours.' Realising she was getting nowhere, Abby propped herself on her elbow and dug Kell in the ribs, trying to inject some humour into this awful situation. 'Did you pick up my suit from the cleaners? We're meeting everyone at the wine bar at seven then on to the theatre, and Reece wants us to meet for eighteen holes of golf on Sunday.'

'Sounds good,' Kell insisted, but Abby shook her head.

'For a holiday perhaps, but you'd end up hating it, Kell, and in turn you'd end up hating me, which I couldn't bear.'

'Don't say that.' He shook his head furiously. 'I could never, ever hate you.'

'Well, maybe hate's too strong a word, but it *would* end up tearing us apart. Tennengarrah's in your blood, Kell, you said it yourself. This is where you belong.'

'But not you?'

Abby shook her head.

'Isn't it worth a try?'

Again she shook her head. 'If it was just about me, Kell, I'd say yes. Even though I've wanted to be an emergency consultant all my life, what's happened between us is so big I actually think I could let it go, give us a genuine try. *That's* how serious I feel about you...'

'But?' Kell's single word was spot on and Abby sat up restlessly. Burying her face in her hands, she massaged her temples as she let out a long, painful sigh.

'All this hot air I've been blowing is starting to take shape.' Looking down, she smiled at his confusion. 'All that tapping away on my computer and firing off emails has finally paid off. My dream's got a name now— EDAP, or Emergency Drug Assessment Programme. Admin's finally come to the party and they're going to allocate funds for one counsellor for a three-month trial. The rapid detox clinic is going to let us have first refusal on a daily bed and I've got more lecturers lined up for the staff than I can count. I can't just walk away now. What sort of message is that going to send?'

'Can't someone else take over?'

She shook her head wearily. 'Oh, Kell, I'm not vain enough to think I'll be the best emergency consultant in the world, that the department's going to collapse if I don't return, but I know for a fact this programme will. Sure, someone might pick up the ball and run with it for a while, but I've called in a lot of favours to get where we are now. If I pull out, how can I blame anyone else for doing the same?'

He didn't say anything and for a while neither did Abby. They just stared into each other's eyes, trying to work out some sort of answer when in truth there wasn't one.

'Anyway…' Abby attempted a grin. 'Given that we've only spent one night together, it might never come to that. Who knows? By the time my contract's up we might be sick of the sight of each other and counting the days until I go!'

Her hollow words didn't even provoke a response, they both knew they were already in way too deep. 'What if you stayed just a bit longer?' The hope in his voice diminished as Abby gently shook her head.

'What would be the point, Kell? The end's still going

to be the same. Let's just enjoy what we have for now, huh?'

'A holiday romance, you mean.'

'A working holiday romance,' Abby suggested, with more conviction than she felt.

'I guess it's an improvement on a one-night stand,' Kell said grudgingly as Abby gave a relieved sigh. 'But I don't want us hiding, Abby. I mean it. There's not going to be any pretending we're just colleagues and scuttling around corners like naughty teenagers. We're on or we're off for the next couple of months, not somewhere in between.' He pulled her closer, if that were possible, breathing her in, revelling in her scent, her presence, before he continued. 'That's another reason I've been holding back, Abby. It isn't just the thought of losing you I can't stand, it's the thought of only having half of you.'

'Why do you think I'd want to hide our relationship?'

'Well, you didn't seem exactly thrilled to have slept with a lowly nurse when you woke up on our first morning together.'

'Oh, Kell,' Abby sighed, appalled at his take on things. 'That didn't even come into it. I was mortified at waking up with someone whose surname I didn't even know, someone I'd only met a few hours before. It was never, ever about that.'

'So I'll do?' A cheeky grin played on his lips, crinkling around his eyes, and Abby fell just a little bit deeper as she gazed back at him.

'I guess you'll have to.' Her answer was casual, flip almost, but the utter adoration blazing in her eyes told Kell she was teasing.

'So no hiding, we're riding back into town as a couple.'

'It looks that way.' Still the casual voice remained, but a bubble of excitement welled inside her, the prospect of going public both thrilled and terrified her—that she could spend her nights wrapped in his arms, awake with him in the morning, come home to him at night. Any hope of remaining casual disintegrated as her lips instinctively moved towards his, desperate to confirm the depth of her feelings with a kiss, but Kell hadn't finished talking yet, the soft smile sliding from his lips as his serious eyes held hers for a moment.

'And when your time's up, Abby, what will we do then?'

She didn't want to think about it, didn't want anything to ruin this precious sweet moment, but deep down she knew there was no escaping it, that the inevitable end would hang over them, not just at tender moments like this but every step of their short way, and some sort of answer was needed. 'Look back with love,' Abby ventured as Kell's eyes shuttered closed for a second or two. 'Enjoy our memories.' Abby managed a quick wince. 'That came out like a holiday commercial. Oh, I don't know, how can I say what it's going to be like? Let's not think about it for now, huh? Let's just enjoy the time we've got, Kell.'

The sky was dark now, a deep indigo, yet she could still see his features, the moon a silver-white ball, the stars multiplying every time she looked, like a million jewels winking and blinking, and Abby felt safe beneath nature's canopy as Kell held her close. As he pulled her towards him, the lips she had missed so much sweeter than her vivid memory, the swell of him against her thigh, nudging higher, parting her womanly warmth, so welcome, so wanted, her hands coiling through his damp black locks, her brown legs wrapping around his hips, breasts swollen and full against his solid chest as words faded away and instinct took over.

Their love-making was as unspoilt and natural as the land that cushioned them, primal and vital in the scheme of things yet so much more than a quenching of primitive desires, than the cocktail of hormones that had catapulted them together that first night. And as wondrous as it had been, it paled in comparison to the reverent way he held her now.

As they made blissful love, as Kell caressed her, not just with his hands but with his eyes, his body, his mind, Abby witnessed there and then the sheer and unequivocal privilege of being a woman.

CHAPTER SEVEN

KELL took Abby home.

To his real home.

A rambling, massive property where Abby met his father, an older version of Kell, with long dark hair greying at the temples, a sun-battered face and a smile that matched his son's. She even forgot to be nervous when Kell held her hand and introduced her to his two brothers, Kane and Rory, whom he clearly adored. And as they all shared a delectable meal Abby bathed in the rosy glow of just being with Kell, learning about him, watching him interact with the family he loved, and the more she glimpsed the more her thirst for knowledge increased, the more she needed to know.

'Can you show me around?' Abby asked as three bikes roared off into the night, a father and two sons, politely choosing tonight to pop down to the local.

No mean feat when it was a half-hour ride!

They drifted outside, following the sound of whinnying horses, hands loosely entwined, and Abby finally worked out why Shelly had laughed at Kell's supposed need for cash. The property reeked of wealth and success and, if it was at all possible, Abby admired Kell more for his nursing work, for caring and sharing his amazing knowledge when he so clearly could live off the land. And though the closest she'd come to a horse had been a donkey ride along Manly beach years previously, despite the fact a horsy person was the last thing Abby would ever be, standing here, the dusty scent of sawdust filling the air, dark faces peering over the fences, excitedly greeting their master, nudging their hands for a treat, for a moment or two Abby almost felt as if she belonged.

'It's beautiful, Kell. Do you use these horses for...?' She gave a helpless look at Kell as she struggled to find the word she was looking for.

'Droving?' Kell replied. 'Not so much these days. A lot of it's done on the bikes now, but for shorter stock routes we still use them. Some of the bigger properties use helicopters.'

'Bigger?' Abby blinked.

'This is nothing compared to some.'

'So do you still go droving?' Abby asked, though really she had no idea what the word even meant.

'Not really. We hire drovers now. The property's doing really well, which inevitably means more paperwork. Kane's still really into it, and Rory heads off more often than not, though he tends to go on ahead and set up camp. Every now and then I get the urge, though, and use up the best part of my annual leave, droving cattle by day and sitting by a campfire at night. Nothing really beats it.'

'I still don't understand what it's for,' Abby said, mystified. 'These stock routes everyone goes on about. What's the purpose of it?'

'To feed the cattle.' Kell patiently explained. 'We move them on to where they can feed. You have to follow the stock routes so they can graze along the way. You should come one time, see it for yourself. Kane often takes tourists out, there's no better way to see the outback.'

She doubted that! An air-conditioned mini-bus sounded a far more comfortable option! Nervously Abby patted one of the more persistent horses, her newfound closeness to nature diminishing rapidly as a pink tongue lolled out, brushing her hand and catapulting Abby back in a fit of nervous giggles. 'I'm not very good at this, am I?'

'You're doing fine,' Kell assured her. 'Though I take it you weren't signed up for the pony club as a child?'

'Afraid not,' Abby admitted. 'I was one of those geeky children who begged her parents to take her to the science museum. Still, it doesn't mean I can't appreciate them.'

'OK, maybe my first suggestion was a bit optimistic, but we really should take a couple of horses out maybe one day this weekend.' He grinned at her startled expression. 'We'd take it gently. I'd really like to show you around the property properly.'

'Maybe,' Abby mumbled. Suddenly thoughts of snakes and spiders were starting to filter in and Kell threw an arm around her as she gave a nervous shiver.

'Come on, you,' he said in that deep, slow voice. 'How about that video I promised?'

'I have to get back,' Abby said reluctantly, as the credits rolled, lingering over a glass of Australian red as Kell lay on the couch beside her, running one lazy hand through her hair. 'I'm on first thing in the morning.'

'Sure.'

She shared his reluctance to leave, felt the coolness on the couch as he stood up. As he pulled on his boots, she glimpsed the domesticity, the sheer luxury of being with him, and shivered at temptation that beckoned.

That with one single word all this could be hers.

A level head was called for, but hard to find, as his bike slid along its dark path, the headlight illuminating fireflies, the night air humming with the wildlife, but this time when they came to Abby's house there were no awkward goodbyes, no nerves at the door, just the delicious feeling of coming home together, the heady excitement as he kissed her, slowly undressed her with his eyes before his hands had even moved, and the slow unhurried pleasure of their love-making.

'Abby, meet me at the clinic!'

The phone had only rung once and in her sleep-fuddled mind Abby struggled to register that it was Shelly speaking on the other end.

'There's been a bus crash. A mini-bus,' she added, and Abby felt momentary relief as the number of potential victims reduced somewhat. 'On the main road into town.'

'How long will it take to get there?' Blinking, she looked at her alarm clock, the numbers flashing three a.m. as Kell jumped up beside her and started to pull on his clothes.

'Half an hour or so. I'm trying to round up Kell— he'll get there more quickly on his bike. Ross is loading up his Jeep and Clara should be just about at the clinic. Jack, the police officer, is going directly to the scene.'

Abby toyed with lying, but only for a second. Lives were at stake and anyway they'd already decided to come out in the open. 'Kell's here,' Abby said, screwing her eyes closed in embarrassment as she held the phone with one hand and pulled on the knickers and shorts Kell was handing her.

'Oh.' The single word said it all, but Abby was saved from saying anything further as Kell grabbed the receiver, enabling Abby to finish getting dressed.

'Ring Ross, tell him to have two emergency back packs waiting. I'll take Abby on the bike with me.'

They roared, literally roared up to the clinic, the adrenaline kicking in, though not enough to completely diminish the cringe factor of Clara's and Ross's open mouths as the new couple so blatantly stepped out.

'How many injuries?'

Ross shook his head, helping Abby on with her massive backpack. 'A truck driver just called through on the radio—at least eight, possibly twelve. The nearest flying doctors are *en route* to Adelaide with a preemie baby so apart from Jack we'll be on our own for a while. I'm going to stay here because the road ambulance is heading out as well so no doubt the victims will start trickling in here soon. Do what you can as first on the scene then get back here. We're going to need everyone on board.'

They fled through the night, the roar of the bike a lonely howl in their mercy dash, and Abby shook with fear, mentally preparing herself for the sight that would greet her, going over and over the basics in her mind. But nothing, *nothing* prepared her for the sight that first greeted them—two massive road trains, their lights blaring and two hulking men flagging them down, their harsh, rough faces choking back tears as they explained that the accident was still a couple of minutes away, their lights a warning to the massive road trains that took this road to slow down, to stop and help…

Because out here a truck driver might be all the help you could get.

The bus was on its side, a gaping, mangled hole displaying the wreck of human life inside, and Abby felt the hot, acid taste of bile in the back of her throat.

Oh, she'd been to numerous accidents, seen more car crashes than she could remember, but she'd arrived *later*, when the firefighters, paramedics and police had secured the area, when her medical brain had been one of many. But nothing on the bike journey had truly prepared her for arriving at this devastating scene an hour after all hell had broken loose…

And being the first medical personnel there.

They bred them tough out here.

Some dad, grandad even, a truck driver, a salt-of-the-earth bloke who should be singing along to the radio or rambling into his CB, was performing CPR on a teenager who should be gossiping, or laughing, or dozing as the mini-bus tore through the endless outback. And Abby knew there and then that the image that greeted her would never ever leave her, would always stay with her as she took in bodies lying strewn on the roadside, moaning, screaming, some sobbing, presumably having dragged themselves out or been pulled out by the truckies who had stopped.

'If they're moaning they're breathing,' Kell called, unstrapping the hard hats from the backpacks and flicking on the torch lights attached to them as he followed some frantic hand signals from Jack and headed for the bus, leaving Abby to make her way over to another truckie still working on the lifeless form beneath him.

As Abby knelt down, hands that should have been shaking were surprisingly steady as she examined the young woman. She held one hand up in the air, the other coming to rest on the truckie's shoulders, feeling the exhaustion, the desperation as he slumped beneath her touch.

'She's dead.'

There was no time for introspection, no time to

close the young eyes or offer a prayer, just on to the next one.

On to a life that could maybe be saved.

Kell wasn't waiting for orders.

Kell was in the bus, giving the kiss of life into a young guy a couple of times then securing a collar around his neck.

'Here, mate,' he called to the truck driver who was helping Abby to climb through a gaping, savage tear in the upturned bus. 'We need to get this guy out now! Abby,' he said, his torch flashing through the twisted wreck onto a pale bloodied face, 'I think that one should be next.'

She heard the gurgle, the horrible chilling sound of the death rattle, as Kell's torch flicked away and Abby jerked into response, the ABC ingrained into her coming to the fore. Clambering painfully slowly over the remnants of life and simultaneously trying not to register that fact, she somehow made it to her patient, her outstretched hands lifting the chin that was falling onto its chest. The light on the top of her hard hat shone onto her patient and Abby saw that the face she held in her hands was that of a young woman.

Sweeping the airway with her fingers, the A dealt with, Abby moved on to B. Placing a resuscitation mask over the slack mouth, she blew into it, relief flooding her as she saw her patient's chest move, the lifesaving breath flooding life into the woman she held in her arms.

'Stay still,' Abby ordered firmly, as she started to come to. 'I need you to stay very still,' Abby said more loudly, as the young woman started moaning and thrashing. Abby held the woman's forehead firmly with one hand as she rummaged in her backpack with the other, only able to finally comfort her patient and introduce herself properly when the cervical collar held her patient's neck safely in line. 'I'm Abby, I'm a doctor.'

'Jessica.' The tiny voice was a most welcome sound and she tried not to think how one minute, two at the most, would have rendered this life extinguished.

Despite the darkness, the unfamiliarity of the surroundings, Abby performed a brief examination, the visible injuries in no way accounting for Jessica's pallor, but as she palpated her abdomen and felt Jessica guard against her touch as she let out a moan of pain, Abby knew the damage was internal. Working quickly, she inserted IV access, tearing at the wrappers with her teeth when no other option presented itself. Setting up the IV fluids, she opened them full bore.

'We're going to get you out just as soon as we can, Jessica,' Abby said comfortingly. 'More help's on the way, but I can't move you by myself.' She deliberately didn't mention the weight of metal pinning the young girl to her seat, the jagged precarious journey Jessica would face to escape from these hostile surroundings. As she heard a whimper behind her, however reluctantly, however much she didn't want to leave this sick, frightened young girl, Abby knew she had to move along to the next unlucky victim.

'If they're moaning they're breathing.' Kell's words rang in her ears as Abby's eyes surveyed the mini-bus, her eyes fixing on a young man who stared back at her with agonised, terrified eyes, and though he was moaning Abby knew he needed help and fast! 'We'll get you out very soon,' Abby said assuredly, as she looked over her patient, words of comfort and reassurance spilling from her lips as she assessed her patient, but her heart sank as her eyes moved downwards, knowing with one awful glance that no amount of modern medicine was going to save this young man's leg. Slipping a tourniquet around his dirty, bloodied wrist and setting up IV access in the back of his hand, she gave a generous dose of pethidine along with the IV fluids which she hung on a gnarled twist of metal above them, only vaguely registering that Kell was back working with her now, which gave Abby some hope that the worse was over.

'What have we got?' Abby asked.

It was the first chance to take stock, the first attempt to formalise a plan of attack, yet still there wasn't the luxury of a calm conversation. It took place as Abby did her best to stabilise the young man's leg while Kell and a truckie struggled to move the weight of steel which trapped him.

'One serious head injury. He's in a bad way, Abby, he needs to be intubated. Clara's just arrived and she's going to do that.'

'What else?'

'Mainly leg and chest wounds. How's the young girl?' He gestured over to Jessica who was ominously quiet now.

'Not good. I want to get back over there.'

'Go.' Kell nodded. 'We're nearly free here.'

Oh, she didn't want to leave this patient, she wanted to stay, to help, to comfort, but three pairs of hands on one body was a luxury they simply couldn't afford here. 'It won't be long now,' Abby said to the young man, before she turned to leave. 'And I'll see you outside very soon.'

Through the twisted wreck Abby crawled, her backpack catching every which way, the extra torch she held in her teeth flashing images too painful to contemplate as she inched her way over, her only comfort the sound of the young man being lifted out of the wreck of the bus.

'Jessica.' Abby pulled an eyelid open, blasted the torch into the girl's eyes. 'Jessica!' she said more urgently, feeling for a pulse as mercifully Jessica's eyes flicked open.

'Get me out of here,' Jessica begged.

'We will, just as soon as we can. There's a lot of wreckage pinning you.'

'I'm going to die.' Jessica was crying quietly now and none of the comforting words Abby attempted worked now as she pushed some refrigerated blood through the IV line, the precious resource desperately needed here.

'This was supposed to be a holiday…' Jessica moaned, her weak voice still managing to portray her mounting hysteria, depleting what little energy she had. 'This isn't what it was supposed to be like…'

'What do you need?' Kell was beside her now but Abby didn't even turn to register him.

'I need to get her out,' she said urgently.

More help had obviously arrived and a portable oxygen cylinder was passed through to them and Abby gratefully placed a mask over Jessica's deathly pale lips.

'I don't want to die here.' Jessica's terrified eyes caught Abby's.

'Jessica.' Abby's voice was sharp now, a mental slap to her patient's pale cheek. 'Listen to me. You are *not* going to die because guess what? I'm not going to let you. Got it?' Her eyes held Jessica's, who mercifully seemed to be calming, but the whiteness of her tongue had a chill running down Abby's spine. 'Get another IV line into her,' Abby ordered, 'and push through some more blood.' But before the words were even out, Abby changed her mind. 'No, I'll do that. Kell, go and get some more hands here. I want her out!'

'It's daytime in England,' Jessica sighed, drifting in and out of consciousness.

'I thought I heard an English accent.' Abby smiled. 'Are you here on holiday?'

'I'm taking a year...' Her voice trailed off and this time no amount of calling her name seemed to reach her and Abby knew time was running out fast. Shouting for help, her bare hands pulling at the seat pinning her patient, Abby struggled to free her, to get her out of this hell hole, to keep the promise she had made...

'The flying doctors are about to land,' Kell shouted through the darkness. 'We're setting up flares along the main road, we can get the head injury evacuated...'

'Jessica's going off,' Abby shouted. 'Get Jack and as many pairs of hands as you can so we get her out, and *then* we'll decide who's going first on the plane!'

Whoever Kell got, they were strong, but even with the three of them it took a superhuman effort to force the seat forward to somehow slide Jessica's body through an impossibly small gap. And as was so often the case, as she slipped out from her tomb Jessica's condition deteriorated rapidly.

'What have we got?' Abby almost wept with relief as a concerned face greeted her, the golden wings pinned to the man's very white shirt the most reassuring sight she had ever seen. 'I'm Hall Jells, the senior medical officer. I think we may have spoken on the radio.'

'Abby Hampton,' Abby said breathlessly. 'Emergency Registrar. Her name's Jessica, that's all I've got. Severe abdominal injures, she's just lost consciousness. She's had two units of blood and a litre of Hartmann's solution, but her blood pressure's still dangerously low. She desperately needs Theatre. I've also done a brief assessment on a young male with a serious head injury—'

'I can only take one,' Hal broke in.

'Take Jessica,' Abby said, painfully aware of Kell's frown as he came over and caught the last of the conversation. 'Hospital's her only hope.'

They liaised for a few moments as they loaded her onto the plane, but as she went to run off Abby turned momentarily. 'She's from England.' Such a paltry summing-up of a young woman, but it was all Abby knew, a tiny personal touch, and as Hall gave her a knowing nod she knew he understood.

'We'll do all we can.'

CHAPTER EIGHT

AT SOME point, night became day, but no one really noticed.

The clinic resembled a war zone, young people fighting for their lives, their limbs, as all around fought with them.

Ross and Abby, guided by the knowing voices over the two-way radio, performed a lifesaving burr-hole on the young man Kell had wanted to evacuate first, relieving the growing blood clot pressing against his brain and giving him a chance at life.

Shelly, who should have been nursing her daughter, snapped into nurse mode and worked alongside Kell and Clara as if she hadn't missed a day, as friends—who anywhere else in the world would be mere neighbours—tended Matthew and Kate.

The whole town pulled together on this black Tennengarrah day. Cups of tea and welcome glasses of water appeared like magic as endless limbs were secured with temporary plaster of Paris back slabs and wounds cleaned and stitched, chest drains inserted and, more poignantly, tears wiped. The flying doctors swooped down intermittently, relieving them of one or two patients, until finally all that was left was a floor awash with bandages, swabs and blood. The exhausted crew, who had been awoken in the middle of the night, had not even paused for breath since.

'Nice work, guys.' Ross stood in the middle, his arm

around his exhausted wife. 'You've all done the clinic proud.'

'Have we heard anything from Adelaide?' Abby asked, taking a long cool drink straight from the tap.

'Hall rang earlier.' Kell's voice made her still and she paused over the tap, dreading what was coming next. 'Jessica had a lacerated liver and a ruptured spleen, along with a perforated bowel. She's in Intensive Care.'

'But she made it out of Theatre.' Hope sparked in her voice and Abby quickly fought to quell it, knowing there was a long, long way to go.

'She made it out of Theatre.' Kell nodded with quiet satisfaction. 'Good call, Abby. I'd have sent the head injury.'

'That would have been a good call, too,' Abby said generously. 'Heaven knows, they both needed help.'

'Well, I for one wouldn't have fancied performing abdominal surgery here. Give me a burr-hole any day of the week.' Ross half laughed.

'If you're so good with a drill,' Shelly jibed, 'how come my shelves are still lying in their boxes on the hall floor?'

'Kell said he'd do them.' Ross gave his wife a playful squeeze around the waist. 'Hey, Abby, are you sure that you don't want to stay a bit longer? Say, a few years?'

There were a few laughs a few 'hear, hear's' but as Abby met Kell's eyes she could see the pain behind his smile, the nonchalance in his actions for once not coming naturally.

'And I thought I was here for a bit of a holiday.' Abby attempted a joke. 'Well, are we going to get this place cleaned up so I can have a long overdue shower?'

'No one's cleaning a thing,' June, who Abby now knew to be the legendary hairdresser's aunt and clinic sandwich maker, said the words with such determination not even Abby would have attempted to argue. 'I'll pull on some gloves and get started, and when you're all rested you can come and finish off. You can't even use the excuse that you've got to restock as you've used all the supplies.'

'Come on.' Kell slung a casual arm around Abby's shoulders. 'I don't know about you, but I'm exhausted.'

Abby's eyes flicked around the room, waiting for a few winks or jeers, but she realised they were all too exhausted to even bother with the latest romance blossoming in Tennengarrah. As tragic as the night's events had been, they'd at least dimmed the spotlight on Abby and Kell.

Almost.

Shelly caught up as Abby wearily signed off the drug book.

'Don't think you're getting off that easily,' Shelly whispered, an impish grin on her usually innocent face. 'I want *all* the details.'

'You bring the wine.' Abby smiled, grateful for the chance of some feminine insight.

'Deal.'

'What are you and Shelly cooking up?' Kell asked as Abby wearily climbed on the back of his bike.

'Girl talk.' Abby shrugged, then smiled as Kell turned around and gave her a quizzical look. 'Whatever that is! I've never really been one for sitting cross-legged on a bed and engaging in a heart-to-heart.'

'Then you don't know what you've been missing!'

'Oh, and you'd know, would you?' Abby grinned, poking a pink tongue out between her lips. 'Being a midwife and everything.'

'So I'm in touch with my feminine side,' Kell said as Abby slapped his back. 'It makes for one helluva lover.'

CHAPTER NINE

FOR a few days at least, Tennengarrah was the talk of Australia.

Or at least it felt that way.

Every news bulletin was filled with images of distraught relatives in England, Germany, Sweden, shell-shocked and stunned as they boarded jumbos, weeping into the cameras, begging their loved ones to hold on till they got there.

Overdressed reporters, who reminded Abby of herself on her first day in Tennengarrah, talked earnestly into the cameras, trying to ignore the flies that buzzed around their heads and landed unceremoniously on their faces as they spoke of the remoteness, the difficult access, the sheer devastation that had struck these unlucky tourists.

But even with the benefit of a script and hundreds of thousands of dollars' worth of equipment, not one of the reporters managed to truly convey the sheer majesty, the grandeur of a land virtually untouched by human hand. Not one of the news bulletins managed to match the image indelibly etched on Abby's mind, the sight she had witnessed as she'd first neared the scene. Not one of them truly portrayed the antithetical sight of the mini-bus, as out of place in this setting as a plastic bag on a deserted beach, the horror of the tourists scattered like dolls on the roadside, the harrowing sight of the make-shift mortuary, or the impressive, anxiously awaited sight of the flying doctors landing their plane on the dirt road, treating the injured and ferrying the wounded.

Restoring order to chaos.

Even the clinic had its share of news coverage. And the lump in Abby's throat, which felt strangely like pride, welled as she replayed her video tape. Minutes of coverage turned into a couple of hours, a legacy of leaping for the remote and pressing the record button every time the news came on.

There was Ross—blond, stunning, articulate, praising his staff.

There was Shelly, pale from combining breastfeeding with a diet, but managing to look like she'd never left nursing for even a second as she bagged an unconscious patient with one hand and spoke into the telephone with the other.

Clara was there, of course, eternally laid-back, completely unruffled—a true outback nurse by anyone's standards.

She cringed as she saw herself, startled by her golden tan, her face void of make-up, tousled dark hair tossed into the scruffiest of ponytails, a far cry from the sleek city girl she was so familiar with, ruing the fact she even cared that her bottom looked massive in her khaki shorts, when beside her Jessica lay a breath away from death's door.

And, of course, there was Kell.

Abby deserved a callus on her index finger for the amount of times she hit the pause button, freezing his image, pausing him in mid-sentence.

And whatever way she looked, he was beautiful.

'Knock, knock,' Shelly called out as she pushed open Abby's front door—about as formal as an entry got in Tennengarrah. Having learned her lesson on more than one occasion, Abby had stopped wandering around her home dressed only in her underwear. Cotton shorts and a crop top—topped with the Akubra Kell had given her—was a far better look than a blushing, eternally embarrassed doctor!

'I was just coming over to see you.' Abby smiled, simultaneously flicking off the video and pretending to be engrossed in a soap. 'Where's Kate?'

'Asleep, and Matthew's having an afternoon doze so I've left them with June for half an hour.'

'You haven't forgotten it's your six-week postnatal check today, have you?'

'No such luck.' Shelly pulled a face and picked up the magazine Abby had discarded on the coffee-table. 'I don't suppose we could lie and pretend I've had it?' she asked hopefully.

'Not a chance. Do you want to head over to the clinic? Or I could do it here.'

'You don't mind? I know Kell's seen more of me than I can even bear to think about, but smiling at him as I head for the treatment room is something I could do without. A girl's got some pride. It's such bliss having a female doctor here.'

'Come on.' Abby stood up. 'Let's get it over with then I can make a coffee or we can have some iced tea I've made.'

'Now you're talking.'

Abby's bedroom had to suffice, and though she was professional, Abby still reeled at the informality of the outback. Postnatal checks with the neighbours while you spoke about the latest lipstick shades were an entirely new ball game.

'All back to normal.' Abby finished, labelling Shelly's pap smear and sorting out her vast doctor's bag which had tripled in size since she'd first arrived in Tennengarrah.

'Not quite,' Shelly sighed. 'I'm still several kilos heavier than nature intended. I'm restarting my diet tomorrow—it's only four weeks till the ball.'

Hardly a ball, Abby thought but didn't say. A massive barn draped in fairy lights more than likely, but it was all everyone in Tennengarrah seemed to be speaking about these days.

'What will you be wearing?'

Abby shrugged. She hadn't given it a second's thought, well, maybe a second. Apparently the men would all be in formal wear and the thought of glimpsing Kell in a suit did strange things to Abby's equilibrium.

'I bought one nice dress with me—I guess it will have to be that.'

'Show me.'

Popping the sample in a plastic bag, Abby went and washed her hands before returning. 'I'll drop this over to the clinic later, it will go on the run to Adelaide tomorrow.'

'If only Bruce knew what was in that little esky he carries.' Shelly giggled and Abby laughed along with her.

They got on really well.

Shelly still burned with shame when she remembered their meeting, insisting she wasn't obsessed with the washing, and Abby burned for other reasons when she recalled that fateful night. Girly chats weren't something Abby was particularly used to, but Shelly was so insistent and so disarmingly nice, Abby's uptight exterior whittled away to zero when she was around. For the first time in her life Abby had a woman friend, someone she could moan to, someone she could gossip with for hours about absolutely nothing, someone to bemoan PMT and cellulite with.

And she loved it.

'Come on,' Shelly nagged. 'Your dress.'

Pulling a white dress out of her wardrobe, she watched Shelly's face for her reaction.

'I love it.' Shelly bounded over, running her hand along the sheer organza. 'Just look at those ruffles around the bust and those tiny straps.'

'Hopefully they'll survive the night,' Abby said, ever practical, but though her next question sounded casual she held her breath as she awaited the answer. 'Do you think it will be all right, for the ball, I mean?'

'You'll be the most glamorous one there. Kell won't be able to keep his hands off you,' Shelly enthused. 'Ooh, look.' Shelly ran an appreciative eye over Abby's dressing-table. 'Gosh, I miss the city sometimes. A quarterly trip into town isn't anywhere near as fun as hitting the shops every weekend, and by the time I've made sure we're stocked up for the next century there isn't exactly time to go make-up shopping.'

'Here.' Pulling open her drawer, Abby tossed a make-up bag to Shelly which she pounced on like an eager puppy. 'It's one of those freebies you get if you spend enough on a bottle of foundation or whatever. I haven't even opened it.'

'You haven't opened it?' Shelly asked, aghast, tearing at the zip like a child on Christmas morning, pouring the countless mini-lipsticks and nail varnishes onto the bed and examining each one with relish. 'And you don't mind?'

'Enjoy.' Abby grinned. 'Six weeks from now I'll be swanning round a department store, ordering facials and massages and getting my nails done. It's the least I can do.'

'Don't,' Shelly grumbled. 'I don't even want to think about you leaving. Why don't you stay a bit longer? Six months at least.' Following Abby out to the kitchen, she perched on the bench as Abby poured two long glasses of iced tea.

'But there's a new doctor coming to take my place.'

'There could be two new doctors starting and we'd still be short,' Shelly pointed out. 'The clinic's really taking off now. Please, think about it, Abby.'

'I can't.' Abby picked up one of the glasses and handed it to Shelly. 'I've got a job, a life back in the city.'

'But it will still be there if you stay a few more months, and you must admit you're enjoying yourself.'

'I am,' Abby admitted without even having to think about the answer.

'And if I remember rightly, there's not too many men like Kell floating around…'

'Shelly.' Abby's voice had a warning note to it. They spoke about Kell now and then—he wasn't off limits exactly, but the inevitable end to the blossoming romance most certainly was. 'Leave it, OK?'

'I can't,' Shelly sighed. 'You clearly adore each other. How can you bear to leave him?'

Fiddling with a lipstick, Abby rouged her lips, determined not to pursue this painful subject, but the chance to talk about it, to glean some fellow feminine insight was simply too tempting, and she gave up on her lips with a low moan. 'Was it hard—for you, I mean?' Abby asked, turning from the mirror, her troubled eyes meeting Shelly's. 'Did you just say yes straight away when Ross asked you to come here with him?'

Shelly nodded. 'I didn't even have to think about it.'

'Well, there's your answer,' Abby said cryptically, as Shelly frowned. 'Maybe Kell and I aren't as serious as you and Ross. I mean, the fact you didn't even have to think about it surely means—'

'It doesn't mean a thing.' Shelly said with certainty. 'Look, Abby, you and I are different. You've got a career.'

'So do you.'

'Not like yours.' Shelly gave a small laugh. 'You're about to become an emergency consultant, for heaven's sake, and you've got that blessed drug programme you're always going on about. I was a reluctant nurse who'd already thrown in her job to concentrate on Matthew. I wasn't giving up a glamorous job I was completely dedicated to. All I had to give up was a whole heap of angst.'

'It's hardly glamorous,' Abby said. 'You should see the department on a Saturday night.' Her smile faded from her face as she carried on talking. 'I just can't do it, Shelly,' Abby said quietly. 'Kell knows where I stand. I've been straight with him from the beginning and he's been straight with me. We both know this relationship isn't going anywhere, so we've just agreed to enjoy what time we've got together.'

She'd said it so many times Abby almost made it sound convincing, but how many nights had she lain in Kell's arms staring out of her window, counting the endless stars in a bid to beckon sleep and wish that she'd signed for twelve months, six even? But to change her contract now, to extend her stay, would only raise false hope.

For everyone.

Oh, she loved Tennengarrah. It wasn't even a reluctant

admission now. Kell had taught her to ride, endless days spent ambling around the bush, picnics by billabongs, listening to the horses whinney as they lay and cooled off in the red dirt, or drank from the water's edge, lying in Kell's arms and trying to hold onto a slice of heaven, trying to pretend it could be for ever.

'I'd best get this over to the clinic.' Putting down her empty glass, Abby effectively ended the conversation, and Shelly gave her a half-smile, concern etched on every feature.

'I'm here, Abby, if you ever need to talk.'

Abby did need to talk, she knew that much. But to whom? Shelly and Kell were hardly objective and her family, when she'd broached the difficult subject on the telephone, had practically choked with laughter at the vaguest prospect of Abby staying in Tennengarrah.

'Thanks,' Abby said lightly, but both women knew it wasn't going to happen. When make-your-mind-up time came, Abby knew she was on her own.

Though obviously thrilled to see her, Kell frowned a bit when she came in. 'Can't you stay away from the place? I thought you were off this afternoon?'

'I'm just dropping a sample off.' Abby shrugged. 'How has it been?'

'Quiet as a mouse. Clara's out on a home visit, then she's going to head straight home and Ross is going out on a mobile clinic. Poor guy. It's a big one today and it will take for ever in this heat.'

'What about you?'

'I'll just twiddle my thumbs here, I guess, in case someone does come by.'

The clinic was supposed to be open till four and though they often worked way past that, sometimes even with inpatients, there was still a measure of guilt in shutting up early, just in case someone was banking on them being open.

'You go with Ross,' Abby offered. 'I can watch things here.'

'You're sure?'

'Of course I'm sure. Anyway, I've got a pile of notes I should have written up ages ago.'

Ross and Kell didn't take much persuading. In ten minutes flat they were out of the door and Abby made herself a coffee, sitting in the air-conditioned comfort of the clinic with her feet up on a stool, actually quite appreciative of a chance to tackle some paperwork.

The silence didn't last long.

'Hi, Abby.' A nervous Martha rapped at the door, then walked in. 'Anyone else about?'

'Sorry.' Abby smiled, putting down her pen. 'Ross is out with Kell, and Clara's gone home early. There's only me here.'

'You're the one I want to see.' Martha perched nervously on the edge of the seat Abby gestured to.

'Trouble with your dad?' Abby asked gently.

'No more than usual. He still refuses to have the operation, still says that he doesn't see the point. Ross came to the house and spoke with him yesterday but Dad's still adamant he doesn't want any surgery and he doesn't want to be resuscitated if anything happens.'

'I heard.' The silence around them lingered for a moment or two as each woman dealt with her own feelings—Martha wondering how she'd cope without her father and Abby wondering how, as a doctor, she could stand by and watch a relatively young man die.

'Anyway, it's me I'm here for.' The words surprised Abby. Though slowly she was being accepted by the locals, a patient actually volunteering to see Abby was a rarity to say the least. 'I know Ross wouldn't say anything, or Kell or Clara, but, well, they're friends, not that you're not nice and everything…' Martha blushed but Abby just laughed away the young woman's awkwardness.

'A bit of distance works wonders sometimes. I know exactly how you feel, Martha. I got the worst case of sunstroke during my first fortnight here and, believe me, coming to on a trolley with Ross and Kell checking me over was just a touch too close to home. Sometimes it's nice just to be a doctor and a patient.'

The ground rules worked out, Martha took a deep breath.

'I'm pregnant.'

Abby didn't say anything, just listened and watched Martha's body language. She was a doctor here, not a friend who leapt around the table and offered congratulations.

'Or at least I think I am. I'm two months late.'

'Have you done a test?' Abby asked, then apologised straight away. 'Silly question. You're not exactly inundated with pharmacies here, are you?'

'That's what got me in trouble in the first place. They sell condoms in the store, but Darlene works there, and Shirley. He could have got some from the pub, but his dad was there.' Her voice was angry and Abby could feel her frustration at living in such a closed community. 'Nothing's private here, but I know that's no excuse for being so careless. I guess you think I'm stupid.'

Abby didn't think that for a second.

Who was she to judge?

After all, Kell's skimpy denim shorts hadn't exactly had room for a tiny foil package and Abby herself hadn't come to Tennengarrah equipped for a night of spontaneous safe sex.

Her period had been anxiously awaited and for once gratefully received!

'My dad's going to kill me, if the shock doesn't kill him first.' The tears came then and Abby sat quietly, opening a box of tissues and letting Martha cry for a while before she spoke.

'Why don't we do a test first, make sure of the facts before we work out what you're going to do?'

Martha gave a watery nod, and took the specimen jar Abby gave her. Abby set about trying to find the pregnancy testing kits, which proved a bit harder than it first appeared. None of the cupboards or drawers held anything and she was half-tempted to give Shelly a quick buzz, but, bearing in mind Martha would be back any second, she didn't want to upset her patient further. Martha might think Abby was broadcasting the news.

She found the tests eventually—locked in the drug cupboard, of course!

Where else would they be?

'It's positive, isn't it?' Martha's fearful voice broke the tense silence.

Oh, it was positive all right. The blotting paper had barely been dipped before a dark pink cross had appeared!

'It is,' Abby said, peeling off another wad of tissues as the inevitable tears came again. 'But it's not the end of the world.'

'Oh, it is, Abby, it really is. What am I going to do?' Martha wailed. 'What am I going to do?'

'Cope.' The one word stopped the tears in their tracks and Martha looked up sharply.

'You'll cope Martha, because if there's one thing I've

learnt in my time here it's that they breed them tough in the outback. The women here can cope with anything that's thrown at them—snakes, bites, droughts, even pink crosses on pieces of blotting paper. Now, first up I'm going to examine you, check that your dates correspond with your size…'

'And then…'

'We'll do nothing.'

'Nothing?' Martha looked up, aghast.

'We'll let the news sink in for a couple of days. At this stage a few days either way isn't going to make much difference. But I have to tell you, Martha, that at this stage of pregnancy a couple of days is really all I can—'

'I don't want an abortion.' Martha's voice was the steadiest it had been since she had arrived at the clinic, and Abby gave a small nod.

'Then you won't have one. But when you've calmed down we'll have a long chat and work out exactly what it is that you do want.'

'I want to have the baby, Des does, too.'

'Des is the father,' Abby checked needlessly, the glow in Martha's teary eyes an obvious indicator. 'And you've both discussed it?'

'It's all we've spoken about for the last few weeks. It's just how we're going to tell Dad that's sending us into a spin. Des is a farmhand. Dad even likes him, which is saying something! But it's going to kill him when he finds out. And I'm serious. Dad could have a heart attack when he hears the news. I'm only eighteen, and if Dad dies, how will I manage? How are we going to cope with the farm without Dad? I need him, Abby, especially now, even though I don't want him to know…'

'Martha.' Abby's voice was sharp, but her eyes were still gentle. Bill's reaction to the happy event had flicked through Abby's mind and Martha had a valid point—given the shape Bill's heart was in, a defibrillator on hand when they broke the news might just come in useful!

'I'll come with you,' Abby said immediately, and Martha let out a sigh of sheer relief. 'I'll even tell your father for you if that will help, but all that is a while away. For now all I want you to do is calm down and for you and Des to get used to the idea that you definitely *are* pregnant, then I want you to come and see me and we'll go through everything from antenatal care to how to tell your father.'

And with that Martha had to make do. As good a doctor as Abby was, there was no magic wand she could wave, no handkerchief to pull out of the hat or puff of smoke that would make the endless problem, faced by women the world over, disappear.

By the time Abby had examined Martha, a cuppa or two shared and the best part of a box of tissues used up, Martha was finally ready to face the world and go home. Abby at last had a chance to tackle her notes, though her mind wasn't really on the job, and she happily put down her pen again as Kell and Ross stomped through the clinic, downing a jug of iced water before they even graced her with a greeting.

'Sorry about that.' Kell grinned, managing to look hot and bothered and sexy all at the same time as he refilled the jug from the tap then banged ice cubes from the tray into it. 'It's boiling out there.'

Kell made way as Ross splashed his face with cold water then went the whole hog and put his blond mop of hair under the jet. 'He's right,' Ross moaned, filling

yet another glass. 'I'd better head off and see how
Shelly's coping. I gave Kate her immunisations today,
and it's hardly the best weather for a febrile baby. I bet
the air-conditioner's struggling to keep up. Any problems while we were out?'

'None.' Abby smiled.

'Any patients?' Ross checked.

'None,' Abby lied, deliberately omitting Martha's
visit. 'Just me and my notes.'

'Well, why don't you head off?' Ross suggested. 'Kell
can lock up, and if anyone comes they can buzz me at
the house. And, by the way, thanks for this afternoon—
it made a helluva difference, having Kell there.'

Now *that* Abby didn't need to be told!

Ross was out of the clinic in double time, anxious to
get back to his beloved Shelly, and Abby fiddled hopelessly with her notes, all too aware that she and Kell
were alone.

'Go,' he said, as he picked up files and pushed trolleys
against the walls. 'I'll just make sure everything's set up
for the morning, or if Ross needs to open up during the
night. You can start the shower running!'

His lazy smile had her stomach in knots, and if it
hadn't been over forty degrees outside Abby would have
run all the way home!

CHAPTER TEN

ABBY needn't have rushed.

In fact, by the time she had showered—slowly—dressed—slowly—and stretched out on the sofa, Kell still hadn't arrived. She didn't meant to fall asleep but only when she heard someone banging around in the kitchen did she open her eyes to the delicious sight of Kell, with a welcome glass of water in one hand.

'What time is it?' Abby asked as the ball of his thumb brushed a piece of sleep out of the corner of her eye.

'Seven.'

'Seven!' Sitting bolt upright, Abby looked around the darkening room.

'Why on earth didn't you wake me?'

'You looked tired,' Kell said easily. 'I thought I'd let you sleep. I've fixed dinner.'

Indeed he had.

A tray laden with huge slices of smoked salmon salad was carried through, followed by crusty damper and a massive jug of lemonade. 'Looks delicious,' Abby murmured, licking her lips appreciatively. 'You spoil me, you know.'

'You deserve it.'

They ate, but for once the silence between them wasn't like the silence of so many carefree, lazy evenings they'd spent together. She could feel Kell's eyes on her, almost taste the tension as he refilled her jug and every now and then opened his mouth to speak.

'What is it, Kell?' Abby asked finally, when she'd

chased the last caper around her plate with her bread and drained the last of the lemonade from her glass.

'What?'

'Something's wrong,' Abby said bravely, more bravely than she felt. Her departure was only a few short weeks away now and serious, in-depth discussions were proving far too painful.

'Nothing's wrong, Abby. In fact, everything's perfect—too perfect, I guess.'

Here it came. Levering herself up, Abby moved from the floor to the sofa, but there was no solace from his gaze there so she rose and padded over to the window, watching the one dark tree on her horizon, the fire of the sunset revving up for its nightly show. She'd seen it, heard it all before and simply couldn't go through it all again.

'Is it so impossible to envision us being together?' Kell asked as Abby let out a slow long sigh. 'I know I'm probably not what you expected in a partner, I know I'm not exactly highbrow, but, Abby...'

She turned, her eyes wide, appalled at what she was hearing, appalled that Kell could even consider the problem was him. 'It's not you, Kell. Hell, you've accused me of being a snob before but surely you don't really think that I'm that shallow?'

'Of course not,' He stood up, walking over to the window to join her, but for once there was nothing confident in his walk, and the hands he laid on her shoulders were loaded with uncertainty.

'Kell, we've spoken about this,' Abby said wearily. 'You know I hate the thought of leaving just as much as you do, but we agreed to just leave it, to just enjoy our time together.'

'That was before.' His black, unreadable eyes met hers then and she felt his hands tighten on her shoulders.

'Before what?'

'Why didn't you tell me, Abby?' Kell rasped. 'You know we can work things out.'

He'd lost her now. Abby stared at him with confused eyes, the conversation truly leaving her behind now, her bewilderment only deepening as Kell took a deep breath and carried on talking. 'I found the test.'

'What test?'

'The pregnancy test. I wasn't snooping or anything like that, but when I was clearing up I saw it as I emptied the bin.'

'It wasn't mine...'

'Well, it wasn't mine or Ross's! Oh, come on, Abby, you said there had been no patients. Look...' His voice trailed off as she started to laugh.

'So this is what the evening doze was in aid of, and making my supper? You thought I was pregnant! Oh, Kell...'

But Kell didn't join in with her laughter, his hurt, confused eyes meeting hers as he checked and checked again that Abby really wasn't pregnant. 'You're sure you're not hiding anything from me?'

'Of course I'm not, so you don't have to worry. Nothing's changed.'

A look she couldn't read flashed over his face—relief, disappointment, she truly didn't know—but as she stood there Abby knew how hollow her words were. She could scream from the rafters that nothing had changed but for an hour or two Kell had glimpsed the possibility of a future, a future that could never be, and losing it was only going to hurt.

She forced a giggle, a bright smile. 'Nothing's

changed,' Abby insisted, and as the ringing phone shrilled it was a laughing Abby that picked it up.

She wasn't smiling as she put it down.

'Bill's on his way in—he sounds bad.'

They ran over to the clinic, an anxious Ross meeting them at the door as he fumbled with the large lock. Pushing in the security numbers on the alarm panel, he briefed them.

'Martha rang. She said that the GTN spray wasn't working, so I told her to stay there, that I was on my way, but, par for the course, Bill insisted that she bring him in.'

Kell was turning on the lights as Abby pulled up some drugs and turned on the oxygen.

'She's only a couple of minutes away. She just rang and said he'd got worse, he's barely breathing.' Tyres screeched outside and the trio rushed to the doors, but Ross put a warning hand on Abby's shoulder. 'No heroics, Abby, just the basics, remember. He doesn't want Intensive Care and he doesn't want to be resuscitated.'

Thank heavens for brute strength.

It took every inch of brawn to carry a limp grey Bill from his vehicle through the clinic as Abby waited with red dots and oxygen mask in hand. Martha was screaming, completely distraught, one look at her father enough to convey the gravity of the situation.

That this was surely the end.

'Don't let him die,' she intoned, clutching at Abby who slipped the mask over Bill's slack jaw, knowing with a sinking heart that his minimal respiratory effort wasn't going to hold out for much longer.

'Please, Abby, don't let him die, not without him knowing.'

Abby's long fingers probed the clammy neck but almost as soon as she located the flickering pulse there she lost it again, and as Bill sank further back onto the trolley Abby looked up urgently. 'He's arrested.'

His chest was so wet with perspiration the red dots wouldn't take, and Abby had to rub his chest with alcohol swabs to enable them to stick.

'Abby.' Ross's voice was sharp. 'Bill didn't want this.'

Looking over at the monitor, Abby saw the wavy irregular line of ventricular fibrillation. A single shock from the defibrillator could make it revert it to normal. A possible miracle was in her hands and Ross was saying no.

'Please, Abby!' Martha was pleading now. 'Do something!'

'Charge the defibrillator.' It took a second to realise that she'd spoken, that the firm, crisp order had actually come from her own mouth, but as Ross shook his head angrily Abby knew that indeed she had, and that, what's more, she was on her own.

'Abby.' It was Kell speaking now, Kell shaking his head as he wrapped an arm around a hysterical Martha. 'Bill knew this would happen.'

'Fine,' Abby said through gritted teeth, flicking the charge switch and placing the gel pads on Bill's chest. 'I'll do it myself. If it's the nurses' board you're worried about facing, Kell,' Abby added, with a slightly bitter note as she carried on with cardiac massage while waiting for the machine to charge, 'I'll take full responsibility.'

She knew she was out of line, knew Kell's reluctance had nothing to do with legalities, but as she shocked Bill, the predicted miracle didn't transpire, and it took three further shocks and a couple of lonely attempts at cardiac massage before Kell reluctantly joined her.

'You don't have to take all the flak, Abby,' he said, placing an ambu-bag over Bill's mouth and pushing oxygen into his lungs. 'We'll share it.'

Ross stood back, his face set in a grim line before he, too, joined them, pulling up drugs and joining in, but from the furious look on his face Abby knew she was in for it.

'I'll explain later,' Abby said, catching his eye for a split second.

'Oh, you can bet on it, Abby,' Ross snarled.

They worked in steely silence, only the harrowing sound of Martha's sobs breaking the bleeps of the monitors, the hiss of the oxygen, the short, sharp, orders from Abby, and when finally the wavy line reverted to a slow but regular rhythm, when Bill's chest rose and fell without the aid of Kell, they all stood back for a moment and watched as Bill started to breathe unaided, watched as he started to slowly come to.

But there was no jubilation, no nods of appreciation or congratulations on a job well done, just the cold morning-after feeling of facing the consequences. As Abby checked Bill's blood pressure, her shaking hand for once couldn't be blamed on adrenaline, just the appalling but unfortunately all-too-regular fear of a passionate decision being dissected in the sterile surroundings of a courtroom.

'My office.'

Abby almost smiled. Ross didn't have an office, just a regular seat in the staffroom, but it was hardly the time to point it out.

'I need to talk—'

'You've got that right at least,' Ross interrupted furiously.

'To Martha.' Abby's voice was surprisingly even as she looked her colleague in the eye then turned to her patient's daughter.

'Thank you,' Martha sobbed, as Abby put a comforting arm around her and guided her away from the trolley where her father lay to the nurses' station, dragging up two chairs and handing Martha a wad of tissues.

'I don't know that your father's going to say the same,' Abby said gently. 'Bill's wishes were very clear, and going against them...'

'I'm his next of kin,' Martha said fiercely, in a surprising show of strength. 'It was me insisted that you resuscitate him, I didn't leave you with any choice.'

Abby shrugged. Litigation was a worry but not a relevant one for the moment. Her problem right now was how to handle Martha, Bill and the jumble that was their lives in whatever time was left. 'What I'm trying to say, Martha, is that at any moment what just happened to your father could happen again. At any moment,' she added, her words hitting the mark the second time around. 'And even if we do attempt to resuscitate your father, this time around we mightn't get him back. If you really do want him to know that you're pregnant, it has to be now.'

'Now?' Martha asked, aghast, and Abby gave a small but definite nod.

'Now, Martha.'

'But it could kill him.'

Abby took a deep breath. Her hands reaching over, she squeezed the icy ones of Martha, trying somehow to inject strength, hope, and then berating herself because maybe there wasn't any to be had.

'Then again, this news might be just what your father needs to hold on.'

Kell gave a small smile as they approached, moving to the head of the trolley to make room for Martha.

'Can he hear?' Martha asked, her eyes darting anxiously to Kell, who nodded.

'He just spoke,' Kell said gently. 'He was asking for you.'

'I'm here, Dad.'

Suddenly Martha looked so much younger than eighteen. She looked like a wary ten-year-old as she grasped her father's hand and struggled not to cry. Abby didn't fare so well, tears quietly slipping onto her cheeks as she watched a child who had lost her mother take the biggest gamble of her life and try to save her father.

'I know you don't want to live, Dad, I know how hard it is for you, but I need you, especially now' Her voice broke and she glanced up at Abby, who nodded for her to go on. 'I'm having a baby.'

For a second Abby doubted whether Martha's words had registered, but as Bill's heart rate picked up and grey eyes that were begging to be permanently closed flicked open, Abby knew that Martha's admission had hit home.

'And I can't do it without you. Des loves me and I love him and we really want this to work, but if I lose you now, if you go and leave me, I don't know how we'll manage…'

Abby placed her hands on the heaving shoulders as Bill's eyes closed again. 'Let him rest now, Martha, he's exhausted.'

'Martha?'

The tiny voice stilled them all but Bill didn't say anything else, just squeezed his daughter's hand tight, and it was Kell who found a chair and placed it at the bedside. 'Abby's right. He needs to rest. Maybe he'll do it better with you sitting beside him, huh?'

'What did Ross say?

Kell found Abby, oh, so much later, sipping coffee in the staffroom and staring vacantly out of the window.

'He made me a coffee then said he'd back me all the way.' Abby gave a small laugh. 'He's great, isn't he?'

'He is,' Kell agreed. 'But I'd give him up for you.' When even that didn't raise a smile he closed the door quietly behind him. 'It was Martha's pregnancy test, wasn't it?'

Abby gave a small nod. 'She didn't want anyone else to know just yet.'

'I understand.' Kell sat down on the sofa beside her, but instead of it comforting her suddenly all Abby wanted to do was cry. 'It was nice, though,' Kell said, his voice pensive, his four little words not needing the further explanation that came. 'Thinking it could be us for a while.'

How did he know?

How could he have known that she'd been sitting there thinking exactly the same thing?

That Abby Hampton, city doctor, almost a consultant, was sitting staring out of a window dreaming of a little scrap of blotting paper turning pink, trying to imagine a life where careers didn't matter, where sleepless nights had nothing to do with the road death toll and everything to do with your own little bundle of love.

They'd make beautiful babies, Abby mused.

An almost consultant and an almost cowboy.

CHAPTER ELEVEN

'I HAVE to go.' Kell's deep voice merged with her dreams and Abby stretched languorously beside him as he brushed her shoulder with his lips. 'Do you want me to set the alarm?'

'Too many questions,' Abby mumbled, pulling his arm back over her and nestling herself back into the curve of his body, feeling the early morning swell of him nudging against the soft inner curve of her thigh. But instead of wrapping his arms tighter around her, edging his body nearer and waking her in the most intimate of ways, he moved, kicking back the sheet and climbing out of bed. Abby found herself frowning into the pillow. 'Where are you rushing off to?'

'I've just got to go.'

He didn't mumble exactly, didn't jump out of bed and pull on his jeans with barely a glance, but the emotional distancing Abby had felt in the past couple of weeks was blatantly evident, and for a while, as she pulled the sheet tighter around her and stared blankly into the grey shadows of the dawn, Abby felt the abyss she had tried to ignore for so long now deepen as Kell stood to go.

'Where?' She held her breath as she said the single word, knowing she had crossed the invisible line they had created between them.

They were two independent people, two stars colliding perhaps, but they both knew their explosion was transient.

Kell belonged here, Abby there, and never the twain should meet.

That was what she wanted, what she had insisted upon, so why was she crossing the line now? Abby tried to fathom as she turned on her side and hit him with the full weight of her question, her hair cascading on the pillow, one glorious pale bosom spilling over the sheet, a stark contrast to the golden shimmer of her arms. 'Where do you have to go? You're not on duty for a couple of hours.'

His eyes couldn't meet hers and Abby chewed her bottom lip as she watched him fumble with the fly on his jeans. 'I just need some space, that's all.'

'Kell.'

Her single word stopped him in his tracks and she watched him hesitate in mid-motion, watched the arms that had been holding her through the night stiffen as he paused, his T-shirt in mid-air, and she waited, waited for him to grin, to catch her eyes and smile that lazy smile, to say 'to hell with it' and climb back into the warm bed beside her and kiss away all the horrible doubts that seemed to be flitting into her mind lately with alarming regularity.

But he didn't.

'What do you want from me, Abby?' Not for a second did he raise his voice, not for a moment did she feel threatened, but so ominous was his tone that for the first time since meeting him Abby felt the sting of his disapproval, the dearth of pain in his voice and she gulped as she tried to answer, but Kell was too quick for her. 'Two weeks from now, you're out of here.' His hand slapped against his thighs and his eyes bored into her as she lay on the bed, naked against this unexpected onslaught. 'Two weeks from now, according to you, I might add, you're going to be right back where you belong. So what's with all the questions, Abby? What's with the sudden need to know my every movement when this time in a fortnight you'll be picking up the pictures and smiling at the memories?' Pulling on his boots, he tossed her an angry glare as she lay there, her eyes wide, reeling from his words.

'Kell?' The question in her voice was evident but the hand that reached out for his was quickly rebuffed.

'What, Abby?' he snarled, but just as quickly as his anger had blown in it seemed to dissipate and she watched as he sat hunched on the end of the bed, his body so loaded with sadness, rejection, despair it made her want to weep. 'I just don't think I can do this any more, Abby,' Kell said in a low hoarse voice. 'I can't just lie next to you and pretend the end isn't going to happen.'

Work was awful.

All Abby wanted to do was to speak to Kell in the privacy of her home, to finish whatever Kell had so unexpectedly started.

Correcting herself, Abby pushed open the clinic door and walked inside. Kell's outburst hadn't been that unexpected. Since the night Bill had become so ill, since the night a baby that hadn't even existed had entered their fragile equation, they had been walking on eggshells, pretending time wasn't racing by, that her departure wasn't imminent...

But, as they knew only too well, ignoring things didn't make them go away. Soon her flight would be waiting, not only waiting but departing from the gate in ten minutes, and could a Doctor Abby Hampton please make her way to the departure lounge as soon as possible.

Ross as usual was in great spirits. 'C'mon, Abby, you've got a mobile clinic this morning. If you want to go to the ladies, make it snappy.'

Feeling like a two-year-old Abby took his advice. Too many times she'd been caught out, and asking Kell or Ross to stop the Jeep wasn't the only indignity one had to suffer in the outback. Thoughts of spiders and snakes and mozzies who seemed to have taken a liking to her were enough incentive to dutifully head off to the ladies' room as Kell moodily loaded up the Jeep.

'How's Bill?' Abby asked Clara as she picked up her bag.

'The same.' Clara shrugged. 'Martha's coming in this afternoon after her ultrasound so hopefully that will cheer him up a bit. I've been trying to get him to talk all night but he's not even attempting to be polite now. Hopefully Ross will have more luck.'

'Let's hope so.' Abby looked over at her patient who met her gaze momentarily, his disinterested eyes flicking away to the bland curtain beside him, and though it hadn't been her intention, though the anger that boiled inside her wasn't aimed at Bill, Abby made her way over.

'So Martha's having her ultrasound today,' Abby said enthusiastically. 'Is she going to find out what she's having?'

So lethargic was his effort it barely merited a shrug but Abby carried on her chatter, refusing to be dismissed, flicking through Bill's notes at the end of the bed as she spoke. 'Your blood work's looking good, Bill. You should be thinking about going home in the next couple of days.'

'I'm too sick.' His eyes didn't even attempt to meet hers and for a moment or two Abby said nothing.

'Then you need to be in a proper hospital, Bill.'

'This is as good as any hospital.' Bill shrugged. 'I get all the care I need here.'

'No, Bill, you don't.' Abby's voice was firm, sharp even, and out of the corner of her eye she saw both Ross and Clara jerk their eyes towards her.

'This is a clinic, an excellent clinic maybe, but it's not a specialist unit. We're here as a holding base, a chance to stabilise patients before they're moved. Neither Ross nor I are cardiac specialists and right now that's what you need.'

'I'm not leaving Tennengarrah.' It was the most emotion Abby had heard from him in days but, as sorry as she felt for Bill, as awful as his plight was, Abby felt angry. Angry that such a young man, with so much to live for, with a daughter that loved him, with a grandchild on the way, could let it all go.

'Bill.' Abby moved closer and though she felt, rather than saw Kell enter she didn't look over, her mind too focussed on this important conversation to let her personal life interfere. 'I'm sorry to say this but, like it or not, you're leaving Tennengarrah.' Taking a deep breath, Abby continued. 'Now, you can leave here on a plane with one helluva lot of hope and a family waiting for you when you get back, or…' The silence around them built for a moment then Abby gave a brief shrug. 'I'm sure I don't have to spell out the other option to you.'

'I'm not going to have an operation.'

'And you're sure, quite sure, that you know what you're saying? Ross has asked me to speak to you again. He says that you're still adamant you don't want to be resuscitated and I have to respect that, so if you want me to countersign his findings then today's the day, Bill. If that's what you really want, then that's what I'm going to do.' Though her pen was poised over Bill's notes she watched her patient closely, registering his muscles quilted around his mouth, a slightly nervous swallow. And though Abby had no intention of signing the papers under these circumstances, Bill wasn't to know that. 'Your daughter needs you, Bill.' She'd said it before, they'd all said it, but this time, for the first time, the words seemed to hit their mark.

'Why would she need me?' Struggling to sit, Bill was the most animated Abby had seen him, but though her heart was in her mouth Abby kept her stance impassive, allowing her patient to continue, knowing it was Bill who needed to speak if ever they were going to get anywhere. 'Why would she need me when all I can do is sit and watch the farm go to pot? If I'm gone she and Des can do something, build it up, make a decent life. I'm better out of the way.'

'He's good, then?'

She watched Bill frown, his eyes confused. 'Who?'

'Des. He's good around the farm?'

Bill shrugged. 'Well, he's a hard worker. Thinks he knows it all, of course.' Realising he'd said too much, Bill lay back on his pillow, but Abby wasn't missing her chance.

'I was like that,' she said, her voice gentler, perching herself on the side of the bed but making sure she didn't get too close. 'I thought I knew it all, too. You saw what I was like yourself when I got here. A city doctor who'd seen it all, sure there was nothing this backwater could teach me. Not that I said it, of course, but I'm sure everyone got the message.

'It's not like that out here, though, is it?' Abby said softly. 'It's beautiful, inspiring, wonderful, but it's a tough old land, and though I've learnt so, so much in the past months I haven't even scratched the surface. It's people like Kell and Clara who teach people like Ross and me, who show us how this land works, how to work with it and sometimes even cheat it.

'They need you, Bill.'

'I'm scared.' A thin, bony hand reached out and Abby took it in hers. 'Scared that if I have the operation I won't wake up. I know it doesn't make sense, I know I need it…' Tears were trickling down his cheeks and he didn't move to wipe them. 'I'm just so scared.'

'I know, Bill,' Abby said gently. 'And I can't give you any guarantees. But if you have the operation at least you've got a chance, and by all the statistics a good one. Bypasses have come on even since you had your first one five years ago. They'll have you walking a few steps within twelve hours, you'll be back here within a couple of weeks. But even without guarantees, it is a chance, Bill, and more importantly it's your only one.'

As Bill slumped back on his pillow, Abby knew better than to push things. Taking on a more authoritarian tone, she stood up. 'I'm not going to sign the order because I think we both know that's not what you really want, but you have to make a choice and soon, or it will be out of both our hands.'

'You did a good job back there.'

It was the first words Kell had spoken to her in the two-hour journey, apart from the odd comment about 'bloody mozzies' or 'stupid cows' that wandered into the path of the Jeep, making the long journey ever longer as Kell, rather less patiently than usual, would get out and give them a hefty slap, moving them on as Abby sat there, wishing this awful morning would end, that she could think of something witty or at least relevant to say.

Something that didn't sound like small talk.

Staring out of the window, aimlessly drinking in each lonely windmill, each thirsty dam Abby wondered how she could bear to leave, and if she couldn't, how she could possibly bear to stay. 'I know how Bill feels,' she said softly. 'I've only been here a while, but I know how hard it is to leave, to think that I'm probably seeing all of this for the last time.'

The silence seemed to go on for ever and Kell didn't even look over, just changed gear for something to do and fiddled a bit more with the air-conditioning, but even as he finally opened his mouth Abby knew what was coming next.

'Bill doesn't have a choice Abby. You do.'

She opened her mouth to speak but Kell beat her to it. 'I'm not asking you to live here for ever, Abby. Hell, I understand about the drug clinic, about your career, but surely we're worth a few more months. Surely what we've had together merits you spending a little bit longer here.'

Oh, it did.

Tenfold, a hundredfold.

But how could she possibly tell him her fears, that another six months beside him, waking with him each morning, falling asleep with him at night, could only make it harder? Make leaving impossible.

'I just can't,' Abby said hopelessly, a paltry return to such a heartfelt statement, and she heard Kell's low sigh of disbelief as he shook his head. 'It's better this way, Kell.'

Thankfully they were professional enough and, perhaps more pointedly, busy enough to put their personal feelings to one side as the clinic got under way. Even though she had only been here a handful of times, already Abby felt accepted, recognising a few familiar faces amongst the patients, working methodically as Kell ran the post- and antenatal clinics alongside her.

'That's looking a lot better.' Smiling as he removed the bandage on Jim's leg, Abby checked the wound thoroughly but there were no signs of infection or inflammation. In fact, the wound had healed way beyond Abby's expectations. 'Maybe Jim can spare me the recipe before I head back to the city because whatever he put on your leg certainly worked.'

As Kell saw his last patient, Abby started to pack up and pulled out the esky, but even the sight of lunch did nothing to whet her appetite, remembering so poignantly their first lunch together, right here in this very spot. Opening up to each other, telling Kell the real reason she was here.

It was hard to believe it was over so soon.

'Abby.' Kell's voice had a ring to it Abby had never heard before, and even before she had looked up her adrenaline was starting to kick in. Between them they had seen some sights over the past months but never had Kell sounded anything other than his usual laid-back self.

It took only a second to realise the cause of his concern. Kell was standing beside a woman and in her arms lay an infant, or at least that was what Abby first thought, but on closer inspection the child lying limp and exhausted in the woman's arms would have been around two, his large dark eyes were sunk in his head, his mouth drooling as he struggled with each breath. As Abby recognized Vella, Kell's arms reached out to take the child from its mother's arms and Abby found her voice.

'Leave him with Vella.' Her words were firm, decisive, and Kell instantly put his arms by his side, a questioning look on his face as he turned to Abby. But there wasn't time to explain. Guiding the woman to the Jeep, Abby felt rivers of sweat running down her back and between her breasts as the direness of the situation hit home.

'Is this your little boy?'

Vella nodded, clutching her child closer, her eyes watching Abby's every movement. 'His name's Billy. He can't breathe.'

'Do you want me to put in an IV?' Kell was pulling emergency trays out, snapping into action, but Abby shook her head.

'No. I want you to get on the radio and get the flying doctors here, a.s.a.p. Kell, tell them we've got a suspected case of epiglottitis.'

She watched as the word registered with Kell, and for a second she was sure he paled beneath his tan, but even before she nodded a confirmation, Kell was onto it, back to the calm efficient bush nurse he was.

'Help him?' Vella's eyes looked pleadingly at Abby and she sensed her impatience.

'Vella, I think your son…' Abby started, but her voice trailed off. There was no place for long words here, their different languages, barely allowing for the briefest of exchanges let alone medical terminology. Vella simply wouldn't understand that one false move, one fright and her child's throat would spasm, blocking off his airway so tightly that even with medical intervention the chance of intubating him would be remote at best. 'Billy is sick,' Abby said slowly. 'We mustn't move him or upset him.'

'They're mobilising.' Kell approached softly, placing one heavy yet reassuring hand on Abby's shoulder. 'Dr Hiller's on the line.'

'Thanks.' Though desperate for advice, Abby stood slowly so as not to upset the child.

'Try not to disturb him,' Abby warned—needlessly, she realised. Now Kell knew the diagnosis he was standing back, letting Vella do all the reassuring. 'Explain to Vella that he needs to be kept calm, that there's a reason why we're not doing anything for him.'

'Sure.'

Their eyes locked for the tiniest of instances and as Kell flashed a reassuring smile Abby was eternally grateful, grateful not just that Kell was here with her but for the blessed fact that today was the day of the mobile clinic, that medical help was actually on hand.

That this little boy stood a chance.

'Have you done any anaesthetics?'

Dr Hiller was straight to the point and Abby was relieved at the absence of small talk instantly, warming to the wise, reassuring voice on the radio.

'I have,' Abby started, 'but not on a child with epiglottitis. The couple of cases I've seen have been with an anaesthetist in the room.'

She was telling the truth. Epiglottitis struck the same fear into doctors as meningitis did into mothers everywhere. Rarely seen now with immunisation, it still popped up every now and then, and Abby, not for the first time, realised the enormity of the work here in the outback, that the massive net they tried to cast was shot with gaping, awful holes, how the very immunisations Vella had reluctantly accepted for her newborn had been missed by this child.

'Don't move him.' Dr Hiller's voice was crisp over

the radio. 'Don't distress him with the portable oxygen or by putting needles into him. Just sit tight and let the mother do all the comforting. It's her you'll need to keep calm, but Kell will be onto that.'

'What if…?' Abby's voice trailed off, knowing the awful answer to her question before Dr Hiller even responded.

'If he stops breathing, his airway will be so swollen it will make intubation almost impossible. Give it one go and if there's no luck move straight to a needle cricothyrotomy or tracheostomy.'

Abby winced into the receiver she held in her hand. A cricothyrotomy or tracheostomy involved making an incision into the patient's throat and establishing an artificial airway, but in a child as sick as this a happy result was definitely not guaranteed. And though, as an emergency registrar, Abby had performed her share of this lifesaving procedure, they had all been done in a well-stocked resuscitation room with relatives safely tucked away and an anaesthetist hot-footing it down the corridor, a world away from this dusty desert and their limited equipment with the child's mother watching her every move…witnessing the last-ditch attempt to save her child's life.

'How long till help arrives?'

The crackling of the radio didn't diminish the direness of the answer.

'An hour.' There was a slight pause as Abby felt the abyss of solitude. 'Give or take, we hold clinics there, so there's no trouble getting in and they're already on their way. Just set everything up as best you can, and if he stops breathing you'll be ready.'

Kell had been busy while Abby had been away. He hadn't put an oxygen mask on the child, but he had placed the tubing over Vella's shoulder, unnoticed by the babe in her arms, and Vella was holding it near her child, hopefully raising the concentration of oxygen he was breathing.

Mike, the mujee, had appeared as if from nowhere, and sat with Vella, patiently talking to her, and Abby was grateful for his presence, knowing that right now he was what Vella needed.

They worked on, only sharing the occasional murmur between them as they opened packs and checked their equipment, but the glance they shared as Abby check the tracheostomy pack was one of pure dread, the outlook, if it came to that, too dire to contemplate.

But for all their internal fears, Vella was only ever the recipient of gentle words of reassurance as they took it in turns to fan her and her child. Billy was leaning forward, his body sagging with each noisy breath, and never had Abby felt more useless, her years of study and practice counting for nothing against this harsh, unforgiving land, waiting with ears on elastic for the low hum of the plane, the only chance Billy really had.

It was the longest hour of her life, the wait interminable, Abby could only liken it to watching some awful documentary, watching a child dying in some remote foreign land and knowing there was nothing you could do. But this wasn't on the screen, this was real life, this was Australia in the twenty-first century, for heaven's sake!

For once even the flies didn't bother her. She barely bothered to flick them away as she took her turn to fan Vella and Billy.

'It's coming.' Mike gave her a reassuring nod as Abby cocked her head.

'I can't hear anything.'

'You won't yet.' He pointed to some birds flying overhead and Abby frowned. 'They know before us.'

Another seemingly tiny snippet, yet again it floored her, all the knowledge, the generations of learning, secrets passed down, ever down. Abby heard the distant hum of the plane, her mouth opening in admiration as she offered up a silent prayer of thanks.

Maybe it was the movement, the sudden lift in tension, but just as they all relaxed, as an end to this torturous time seemed in sight, Abby saw the child lie back a fraction in his mother's arms. Vella simultaneously let out a low moan of terror. Billy's colour, never particularly good, seemed to be grey now, the life force draining out of his tiny body. Abby rued the second she had relaxed and Kell, in one movement, took the limp body from Vella, laying the toddler on the rug at the back of the Jeep as Mike took the weeping woman to one side, his dark, knowing eyes catching Abby's. She felt the weight of modern medicine fall to her shoulders as she felt the tiny lifeless form beneath her hands.

Kell deftly slapped the back of Billy's hands to bring up the veins, finally getting IV access into the child, pushing in the antibiotics they had already pulled up and connecting a flask of fluids as Abby placed an ambubag over Billy's slack mouth and tried to push oxygen into his lungs.

They had both set up for this moment, formed a plan of attack should the worst happen, but the resistance in the bag told her she wasn't getting anywhere, and with a frantic shake of her head she looked over at Kell who passed her the laryngoscope—the curved torch that would act as a guide to the tube Billy so desperately needed to help him breathe.

'I can't see anything.' Abby's voice trembled as she

peered into the child's throat, trying to visualise the vocal cords, but Billy's throat was too swollen, making any hope of passing the tube impossible.

The seconds that had ticked by so slowly for the past hour were suddenly whizzing past at an alarming rate, every second moving them unwillingly closer to the three-minute mark that would mean this little boy would suffer irreversible brain damage.

'They're coming.' Mike's voice was jubilant, hopeful, but both Abby and Kell knew his hope was false, that even if they ran like Olympic sprinters from the plane they would be too late.

Resuming the bagging Abby shook her head as she saw his rapidly decreasing oxygen saturations on the portable monitor. 'I'm going to do a cricothyrotomy. Pass me the twelve-gauge needle.' Abby's firm voice belied the appalling sense of dread in every fibre of her being, her one last shot at getting vital oxygen into the little boy.

Vella's screams multiplied as she watched Abby prepare the neck with a swift swab of Betadine, the pitiful wails causing a flurry of activity in the trees around them, startled birds flitting away, but it all went unnoticed by Abby, every cell in her being focussing on the little boy before her as she felt for the correct area in his neck, felt her way with trembling fingers and then held her breath as she pushed the needle in, dissecting the swollen tissue, the tiny space the needle created allowing a hiss to escape as Abby let out the hot air she had been holding in her own lungs.

'Come on, Kell,' she snapped, as he pushed together the connections, the harshness in her voice not even meriting a glance. No criticism intended and none taken, just a desperate attempt to save a life. He connected the tiny airway she had created, no wider than an intravenous needle, to the oxygen tubing, and this time, when Abby squeezed the ambu-bag gently, she watched with sheer relief as Billy's chest moved, colour slowly returning with each gentle push of the bag.

'His oxygen saturation is coming up,' Abby said, glancing at the tiny portable monitor. 'This will at least hold him until…' She didn't finish the sentence, the sight of the flying doctor team descending upon them the sweetest she had ever seen.

'We meet again' was the only greeting Dr Hall gave as he set to work, checking his patient, listening to Abby's handover as his nurse worked alongside him, passing him the equipment he needed as they secured Abby's handiwork, stabilizing the little boy before moving him to the plane.

'Dr Abby?' Mike came over, his face almost obliterated by a huge bushy beard, but there was no mistaking the gratitude in his eyes as he shook her hand. 'This is your last clinic?'

'Yes,' Abby said simply, not quite ready for the first round of goodbyes yet knowing they had to be faced.

'Thank you.' His hand reached into his pocket and, pulling out a glass jar, he handed it to Abby, his dark hands closing around Abby's for a moment, the significance of his gesture bringing tears to Abby's eyes as she looked at the muddy lotion in the bottle.

'Billygoat weed.' Abby smiled through her brimming eyes. 'I'll use it wisely. And thank you, too, Mike. I've learnt a lot from you.'

And then he was gone, back to where ever he'd come from, and Abby stood there, holding the treasured glass jar in her hand. She was barely able to answer as Kell broke into her thoughts with a slightly gruff voice, the inevitable farewells undoubtedly painful for him, too. 'Dr Hall's ready to move Billy.

'We've taken bloods and given him his first dose of antibiotic,' Kell said to Dr Hall, his voice resuming its more usual nonchalant tones as the team gently moved Billy onto a stretcher. Abby carried the IV flask as they headed for the plane, with Kell relaying all the drugs that had been given as if he were reading off a shopping list, the emotion gone from his voice now, back to the unflappable bush nurse Abby knew.

Loved.

Now order was restored, now a life wasn't balancing on a knife edge, that word popped into her consciousness again, knocking her sideways with its impact, taunting her with the impossibility of the match.

'You did pretty damn good there, Dr Hampton.' They were both shielding their eyes, watching the white plane winging its way through the blue sky, carrying its precious load. 'And without a radiographer or path lab in sight. You saved his life,' Kell said more insistently when Abby didn't respond, wrapping an arm around her and pulling her towards him.

'We did,' Abby corrected, but Kell wasn't having a bar of it.

'No, Abby, you did. The second you saw him, you knew what was happening. It was you who told me to leave him with his mum, not to touch him, not to upset him.'

His words hit home and it was then Abby realised how far she had come, how right Reece had been to send her, that Tennengarrah had been a learning curve she had needed to explore.

'Let's get you home, huh?'

Home.

Climbing into the Jeep, Abby rested her head against the passenger window, and this time as she gazed out of the window it wasn't aimlessly. This time she tried to capture each image, to relish it, to save it, to hold it in her heart for ever and wondered why she had to feel this way.

Why the word 'home' couldn't conjure up for her endless red earth dotted with white weatherboard houses, why it didn't signify tired, lonely windmills working woefully empty dams. A career was there for the taking, one where she could make a real difference.

And for the hundredth time in as many minutes she wondered what was wrong with her. Why the sterile anonymity of a concrete hospital and the pressures of dealing with drug addicts held more charm than the medicine she was practising here. Why the creamy sails of the Opera House seemingly billowing across the harbour filled her mind when she thought about home. Why walking unnoticed along a crowded street with shops and cafés held more charm than the life she could lead here…

If only she would stay.

Kell sensed her pensive mood and drove along in silence, idly humming along to his favourite CD. Even when they pulled up at the clinic, laboriously restocked the boxes and refuelled the Jeep, filled in Ross on the day's events and headed for home, there was no idle chit-chat, just a loaded sadness as she pushed open her front door.

'I'll say goodnight, then.' She heard the uncertainty in Kell's deep voice as her eyes shot up, startled.

'Where are you going?'

Soft lips met hers briefly, the scratch of his cheeks brushing against hers as he pulled away. 'I know this is hard for you, Abby, it's hard for me, too. I can understand if you need some space. Anyway, I've got to be up early.'

'You're not on duty tomorrow.'

Kell shrugged. 'I'm hitching a ride with Bruce. I've got a few things to do in town.'

'Oh, Kell.' Her eyes sparkled with tears and she squeezed them closed. The thought of one night apart from him sent her into a spin of uncertainty, yet here she was checking out for good, signing up for a life without him. 'I don't want you to go, that's not what this quiet mood's about.'

'You don't?' Hope sparked in his eyes, that lazy, familiar smile spilling onto his face and Abby didn't even try to resist the urge to reach out and touch him, to somehow capture his smile in the palm of her hand.

'I don't,' she said, her word muffled by the weight of his kiss.

But even as they drifted towards the bedroom, even as he laid her down and kissed her as only Kell could, as their bodies mingled with the infinite desire they ignited, the tears still sparkled in her eyes.

The weight of his body as he lay on top of her, the silhouette of his shoulders as he moved inside her, the feel of that dark tousled hair beneath her fingers, the scratchy maleness of his thighs as they moved against her were all captured in the glistening pools of her eyes, as something deep inside told her to treasure this memory.

And later, as he held her, snuggled into her and slipped one arm under her then cupped his other hand over her breast as he drifted off to sleep, the tears that had threatened all day fell, sliding into her hair as she recalled the bitter-sweet memory of their love-making.

Sweet in its perfection.

Bitter in its finality.

CHAPTER TWELVE

'COME on, lazybones!'

Peering around her front door, Abby blinked a few times at Shelly, running a sleepy hand through her tousled hair. 'What time is it?'

'Ten a.m.,' Shelly said in a matter-of-fact voice, pushing open the door and marching inside leaving Abby to wince at the bright sunlight, close the door and follow her through to the kitchen.

'Is there a problem at the clinic?' Abby asked, perching on a barstool and trying desperately to wake up properly. 'Only Kell left at the crack of dawn, so if you're looking for him…'

'No,' Shelly answered cheerfully, depositing a large bag and simultaneously filling the kettle. 'It's you I'm after. In fact, I've even got a bit of gossip, but it's the ball tonight that I'm really here about. We've got to go to the hairdresser's.'

'Now?' Abby protested. 'But it's the crack of dawn.'

'Hardly!'

'Believe me,' Abby mumbled, 'on my day off, ten a.m.'s the crack of dawn.'

'Well, we were lucky to get in. There are about one hundred and fifty women all wanting their hair done today. It took a hell of a lot of sweet-talking to get an appointment. She's even going to do your nails.'

Abby glanced down at her hand, weakening at the thought of a manicure. The French polish she had arrived with had long since depleted.

167

'So how did you get her to agree?' Abby asked, half yawning and wishing the kettle would hurry up.

'Never you mind,' she said lightly as Abby's eyebrows furrowed. Shelly was up to mischief, Abby just knew it. 'Let's just say I've got contacts. Now all we have to worry about is looking beautiful. I just wish I'd taken my diet a bit more seriously.'

'Don't be ridiculous,' Abby admonished. 'You look great.'

'Exactly,' Shelly sighed.

'I meant you look wonderful.' Abby grinned. 'For someone who had a baby ten weeks ago you're looking amazing.'

'Amazing's the word,' Shelly moaned, depositing a steaming mug in front of Abby. 'Did you know you can actually get stretch marks on top of your old stretch marks? My rear end looks like a map of Australia.'

'And we all know how patriotic Ross is.' Abby winked, perking up as she took a few sips of coffee. 'So, what's the gossip?'

'Your replacement's arrived!'

'My replacement?' Suddenly Abby didn't feel so perky any more. Instead, she felt twitchy and threatened, but she kept her smile in place as Shelly continued.

'He's two weeks early. Apparently he ran out of money in Coober Pedey, though how anyone can break the bank there beats me! You're supposed to make your fortune there fossicking for opals. Heaven only knows what he spent it on.'

'What's he like?'

Shelly gave a small sigh. 'English, very English. His name's Timothy, not Tim or Timmy but Timothy, and even though I'm an exceptionally happily married woman, I have to admit he's gorgeous.' Shelly let out a shriek of laughter. 'And the best bit is, I'm not the only one who thinks so.'

'You've lost me,' Abby admitted.

'You should have seen Clara blushing. I'm serious!' she exclaimed as Abby gave her a disbelieving look. 'Ross can't believe it either. I mean, Clara's just Clara, salt of the earth, never in a flap, but she was blushing to her roots and dropping things all over the place when Ross showed Tim around this morning.'

'Timothy,' Abby corrected, standing up and draining the last of her coffee. 'So who's going to look after the clinic tonight? Bill's still hanging in there, I assume.'

Shelly nodded, but again Abby found herself frowning, sure she had seen a tiny blush grace Shelly's cheeks. 'Ross really thought you'd hit home with your pep talk but I'm afraid he's still staring at the curtains and sinking further and further downhill. Anyway, Ross has asked Noelene Barton to fill in for tonight. I doubt you'll have met her, she's not exactly sociable, but she's a registered nurse and every now and then, at Christmas and the like, she does a couple of shifts to keep her registration up. She's going to babysit the clinic.'

'And who have you got lined up—for Matthew and Kate, I mean?'

'No one.' Shelly grinned. 'That's the best bit about this place. I'll bring the kids and I probably won't see them all night, there'll be a million and one women clucking over them like broody hens. And the best bit of all...' She gave a cheeky wink. 'By the time we get home, they'll both be so exhausted they'll sleep the entire night through.'

'You scarlet woman, you.' Abby grinned.

Whatever clout Shelly had by being Tennengarrah's loyal doctor's wife, she'd certainly used it today. June's house was a hive of activity but all the grey roller-haired ladies parted as Abby and Shelly walked in, and instead of protests they smiled affectionately as Abby's hair was curled around yellow and pink foams. Not even the slightest murmur of disapproval went up as Abby was privy to the one and only manicure of the day.

'I can't fit you in again this afternoon so you'll have to do the rest yourself. I need you to take the curlers out an hour before the ball,' Anna the hairdresser instructed in such a serious voice Abby wondered if she was about to be asked to sign a consent form! 'But you mustn't brush your hair, that will make it all go frizzy. Just put a dash of the serum I gave onto your hands, work it through your fingers and run it through the curls. They should fall beautifully.'

'Th-thank you,' Abby stammered as the whole room looked on.

'And try and let your nails dry for at least an hour before you do anything. You don't want any dints in your varnish.'

'Of course not.'

Only then did it dawn on her, looking around the smiling faces, the nudging going on behind the occasional magazine, that her preferential treatment had nothing to do with being the locum doctor, nothing to do with Shelly and her 'contacts'.

It had everything to do with Kell.

His early morning dash with Bruce was starting to make sense now, and as they paid and left Abby couldn't wait to get Shelly alone and confront her.

'Where's Kell gone today, Shelly?'

'How should I know?' Shelly strode on, the blush on her cheeks only confirming Abby's suspicions.

'Because the whole of Tennengarrah does,' Abby

snapped, as Shelly finally slowed down. 'That's what this is all about, isn't it—the hair, the nails, Kell disappearing to ''pick up supplies''? What on earth was he thinking?'

'It's not Kell's fault.' Shelly swung around, a sight for sore eyes in massive rollers. 'He hasn't said a word. It was Bruce who mentioned…' Her voice trailed off but Abby wasn't going to let her leave things there.

'What exactly did Bruce mention? Come on, Shelly, I need to know.'

'Kell went into town a couple of weeks ago. Bruce saw him in the jeweller's, that's all, and Kell asked to go back today. Bruce thinks it's to pick up a ring. It's all hearsay, Abby, but it doesn't take much for word to get around here.'

'He's going to ask me to marry him.' The shiver in her voice was one of pure amazement. Even though she had suspected it, saying it felt completely different.

'He loves you, Abby.' Shelly took a couple of anxious breaths, 'This surely can't come as that much of a surprise,' she said. 'Please, please, don't let on I've said anything.'

'Just so long as you don't say anything else.' Abby's mind was whirring, the need to be alone, to think things through overriding politeness for now. 'I mean it, Shelly, don't say a single word to anyone.'

Anna had been right. Her hair did fall beautifully, but as Abby stared into the mirror, her snaky dark ringlets hanging over her shoulders, the white ruffles of her dress accentuating her tan, Abby barely recognised herself.

But it wasn't the coiffed woman staring back at her that was so unrecognisable, it was the very fact she was actually seriously considering staying, breaking her promise to David, throwing every professional dream she had held dear for so long now away in the name of love.

A whole afternoon wrestling with her soul had made the picture no clearer, and as Abby walked past the clinic the weight of indecision made her linger a moment, peering into the windows and trying to picture herself there. The sight of Ross, dressed to the nines in a dinner suit, though, wasn't one Abby was expecting!

Pushing the clinic door open, Abby made her way to the small ward, a questioning look on her face as she walked over. 'What are you doing here?'

'I could ask you the same.'

Abby gave a small shrug. 'Kell rang. He got held up with Bruce, but he's on his way back. He said he'd meet me there. What's your excuse?'

'Your pep talk with Bill worked. He's decided to have the operation, so I called the hospital and they want him there tonight—there's been a cancellation and there's space on the theatre list on Monday. We've been waiting all day for the flying doctors but they just rang through and should be here within the hour.'

So Shelly had been lying! 'Can't Noelene deal with it? I thought she was looking after the place tonight.'

Ross gave a tight smile. 'She's making a cuppa. And Bill needs to be handed over properly. It's not fair to land it all on Noelene.'

'Or Shelly,' Abby exclaimed. 'Shouldn't you be over there admiring her new dress, telling her how fabulous she looks?'

'Don't make me feel worse,' Ross groaned. 'Hopefully they should be here soon. Shelly's putting on a brave face but I know she's been looking forward to tonight.'

'Go,' Abby said as Ross gave her a wide-eyed look.

'I mean it, Ross. Shelly's been looking forward to tonight for ages. I can take care of Bill.'

'But what about you? What about Kell's...'

Abby shook her head as Ross's voice trailed off.

'Kell's plans for tonight,' Abby ventured as Ross winced in embarrassment. 'Don't worry, Ross, I had already worked it out for myself.'

'So why are you putting your hand up for an extra shift?' Ross asked perceptively, his grin disappearing as Shelly answered, her voice was thick with emotion, black, mascara-laced tears slipping down her cheeks as she rummaged in her bag for a tissue.

'Here.' Ross pulled a wad from the box on the desk, a startled note in his voice as he watched his crisp, efficient colleague dissolve into a mass of tears. 'I'm sorry, Abby. I was only joking, I didn't realise there was a problem.'

'There shouldn't be,' Abby sniffed. 'We love each other, I know that more than I know anything.'

'So what are you so scared of?'

Abby took a deep breath, her eyes finally dragging up to Ross's, who waited patiently as she struggled to answer. 'I'm scared that when Kell asks me to marry him, I'm going to let my heart rule my head and say yes.' Ross looked at her bemused as Abby cried harder. 'It could never work, Ross, it's just all too hard. Kell's not going to leave here, he told me the first night we met he couldn't even consider it, that Tennengarrah's in his blood...'

'But not yours,' Ross finished for her gently.

'Not mine,' Abby said sadly. 'Oh, I've grown to love it. I love the people, the work. If anything, I've enjoyed practising medicine here more than I ever have in the past, but I just can't stay here for ever. I've got com-

mitments in the city, promises that need to be kept, and
if I agree to marry Kell I'll be letting so many people
down.'

'Yourself included?' Ross asked gently.

'Myself included.' Abby nodded. 'Look, I know the
work I do in the city isn't everyone's cup of tea but,
Ross, it's something I really feel I have to do. If I let it
go now, some time in the future I know I'm going to
regret it.'

Ross looked at her thoughtfully for a moment before
speaking, his knowing eyes surprisingly understanding.
'Which is no way to start a marriage.'

Abby nodded glumly as Ross continued gently.
'Sometimes you can think about things too much, Abby.
Shelly had a home, a life, a family in Melbourne, a special needs child and an ex-husband to boot. If we'd really sat down and thought about the logistics of packing
up and moving here, we'd probably never have made it.'

'So why did you?' Abby asked. 'What made you do
it in the end?'

'I loved her,' Ross said simply. 'And I loved Matthew
and I loved Tennengarrah, so I really hit the jackpot
when I got all three wishes granted.'

'You did,' Abby said softly. 'But, then, you knew
what you wanted, Ross. If a genie popped out of a lamp
now, I don't know what my three wishes would be.'

'Some space,' Ross suggested gently, and after a moment's deep thought Abby nodded slowly, scarcely able
to believe her ears as Ross offered her an out. 'There's
a plane landing soon and it's heading for Adelaide.
Maybe they can make room for a doctor on board, a
doctor heading for home.' As Abby swallowed hard,
Ross continued, passing endless reams of tissues as he
did so. 'You can get a connection to Sydney ,when

you're there, even if you have to sleep on the airport
sofas for a while. Look, I'm not one for goodbyes, either,
Abby, and with the whole town watching you two tonight, waiting and watching Kell's every move, I can
imagine the pressure you're under. If you want to go
now, I'll understand.'

'But my contract—'

'Timothy's here now, and he's more than happy to
start working.'

'What will you tell Kell?'

'That Bill needed a doctor escort. I'll tell him the truth
when the ball's over.'

'Shelly will kill you,' Abby warned, but Ross begged
to differ.

'Shelly will understand.'

But still Abby didn't get it. 'Why would you do this
for me, Ross? Why would you take all this on?'

'You delivered my daughter, Abby,' Ross said slowly.
'A breech birth in the middle of nowhere. We both know
how awful that could have been. You're an amazing
doctor and, given the chance, you'd have been an amazing friend to Shelly and me. I reckon I owe you at least
this.'

It didn't take long to pack, Tennengarrah wasn't exactly lined with shops and Shelly had lightened her of
every last scrap of make-up. Abby's case snapped closed
with surprising ease. The only extra thing she took was
the rather battered dusty old hat Kell had given her, and
as she pulled it on her head, Abby heard the buzz of the
plane, the lights filling her empty living room for a second and as it swooped in for landing, she screwed her
eyes closed and mentally begged for Kell's understanding, for him to know that even if she was taking the

supposedly easy way out, every last step was loaded with agony.

'All ready?' Ross met her outside the clinic, took her computer and wheeled the suitcase the last few steps as Abby struggled to hold back the tears.

'Where's Martha?' Abby gulped, looking around through tear-laden eyes as they loaded Bill onto the plane.

'She can't go, that's one of the reasons Bill found it so hard to make the decision. It's a long, lonely day in hospital when you know you're not going to get any visitors. But Martha needs to stay and look after the farm and in the long run that will give Bill more peace of mind. They were both getting too upset saying goodbye, so Dr Hall suggested that she race home and put on all the lights. They're going to fly low over his property so he can see it again.'

Any chance of a controlled goodbye dissolved there and then as a new batch of tears burst forth, and for a moment or two Abby struggled to catch her breath.

'Come on, Abby.' Dr Hall's voice was kind but firm. 'Ross has got a ball to get to.'

'You've got your first wish.' Ross gave her a quick hug and as she stepped onto the plane Abby turned.

'When I've worked out what my second one is, I'll let you know.'

'You can do a ward round when we get to Adelaide,' Dr Hall grinned as he sat down next to her and clipped on his seat belt. 'There are a couple of patients doing very nicely there, thanks to you.'

'Jessica?' Abby asked, and Hall nodded warmly.

'She'll be going home in a couple of days. Well, not to England, but her parents have flown over to be with her and they're going to have a nice gentle family holiday before they all head back. And the little tacker with the epiglottitis is doing well. He's off the ventilator and they're trying to wean him off his tracheostomy.

'You've been an asset,' he added warmly. 'We're sorry to lose you.' He busied himself then, politely not noticing her tears as he concentrated on his notes in front of him as they flew out of Tennengarrah, the plane flying even lower as they passed over Bill's property. Abby held his thin hand tightly as he leant back on the stretcher gazing out of the window into the darkness, the lights blazing their goodbyes down below. Holding back her tears was the hardest feat Abby had ever undertaken, but this was Bill's goodbye, not hers. And when the last light had disappeared, when just the endless night sky surrounded the windows, he leant back further on his pillow, his scared, sad eyes meeting Abby's.

'I'll see it again, won't I?' His weak voice was barely audible over the engine, the oxygen mask over his face forcing Abby to lean forward to catch his words. 'This isn't the last time, is it?'

Smiling bravely, Abby leant forward, squeezing his hand ever tighter. Her voice was so positive, so assured and full of hope, even Abby wondered where it was coming from. 'You're doing the right thing and you *will* see it again, Bill. This isn't goodbye.'

Comforted, reassured, his anxious eyes closed for the bliss of sleep as Abby sat dry-eyed beside him, not even attempting small talk with the busy, efficient staff and wishing, wishing more than she ever had before, that someone, anyone, could say the same words to her.

CHAPTER THIRTEEN

'THIS coffee's disgusting.'

As Abby walked into the staffroom she looked at the gathered night staff, grabbing a quick drink before the Saturday night shift started and she managed a rueful smile. Gone were her insecurities, the paranoia that the conversation shifted each and every time she entered the room.

The coffee here *was* disgusting and, as Kell had pointed out, it really was all that was on the nurses' minds.

'Then it's just as well I've been shopping,' Abby said, pulling a massive jar of the most expensive instant out of her bag. She pulled a marker pen off the whiteboard. 'That should keep the hordes off,' she said as she placed it on the coffee-table.

'It will, too.' Jane, the night charge nurse, grinned as she read Abby's bold writing. '"Hands off! Abby Hampton, Consultant." Present company excepted, I hope?'

'Absolutely,' Abby said as she checked in her pigeonhole and pulled out a few manila envelopes. 'Finally,' she groaned, as her new name badge fell into her hands. Clipping it on, the one she'd waited so long for, Abby accepted the trickle of applause that went around the room.

'So it's finally official,' Jane cheered. 'Our Abby really is a consultant.'

'So it says here.' Peering down at her white coat, the sense of anticlimax surprised even Abby.

She'd been back a fortnight now. Visited the Opera House, taken a ferry across the harbour and lain on Manly beach, walked around the Botanical Gardens, slipping off her shoes and revelling in the soft damp grass beneath her feet. Been to the theatre, eaten authentic Thai Tom Yum and Japanese Tepanyaki Beef on various nights with the best of them as her colleagues had toasted her success, shopped till she'd dropped and had more than her share of facials and massages.

Everything she'd missed, everything she'd wanted, there for the taking now.

And it didn't mean a thing.

Only work was her salvation, the one real pleasure she had. Nothing, not even a tourist bus crash, or a child with epiglottitis in the middle of nowhere, quite made up for the thrill of promise that filled city emergency rooms the world over as they prepared for a Saturday night.

It was either there or it wasn't.

You either got it or you didn't.

But as she pulled her stethoscope around her neck, clipped her pager in her pocket and walked through the already steaming waiting room, past the 'Staff Only' doors and into the pulsing hub of activity on the other side, Abby knew that work alone wasn't enough.

That love had won.

Oh, she wasn't about to down tools and leave, the drug programme was too precious to abandon at this fragile stage, but, then, so was her relationship with Kell. Abby's hand dug into her pocket, her fingers closing around the half-finished letter she had written. Hopefully she'd get the time to complete it on her break tonight, that she could somehow translate the jumble of thoughts in her brain into a semblance of a letter. That she was sorry she had left, but not sorry she'd come back. Sorry for the pain she had caused. But could she ask for a favour?

Was a year too long to ask Kell to wait? A year to get the programme running, a year to see things through...

'We're down two staff,' Jane said briskly, handing Abby a mountain of patient files. 'We've only got one nurse really qualified for resus at the moment.'

'What about you?'

Jane gave small shrug. 'I'm in charge, so officially I don't count, but, of course, if something comes in I'll just have to split myself in two, or three,' she muttered as the emergency bell went.

'No.' Abby shook her head firmly. 'Get me the supervisor on the phone and I'll have a word.'

'Done,' Jane barked as she shooed out a couple of drunks who had wandered through. 'There's not a nurse on the wards prepared to come down, so they've agreed to send an agency nurse.'

'Great,' Abby muttered.

'Don't shoot the messenger.' Jane grinned. 'Who knows? The agency might get it right for once and send someone who's actually done emergency and not a poor woman who's spent the last decade nursing geriatrics!

'It looks like you're wanted,' Jane sighed, relieving Abby of the notes and gesturing towards resus. 'Roll on seven a.m.'

'Wanted' was an understatement. A grad nurse was attempting to stop an elderly man strapped to a cardiac monitor from climbing over the cot sides of his gurney as Haley, the sister down for resus, set up a bed and started to pull up drugs.

'What's coming in?' Abby asked, getting straight to the point as she pulled on some latex gloves.

'Query heroin overdose,' Haley said, filling up a syringe from a vial. 'Security just alerted us. His so-called friends just dumped him in the car park. Uh-oh.' Jane's face at the door didn't bode well.

'Ambulance Control just radioed through. They're bringing in a motorcyclist with major head injuries. I've paged the trauma team and they're on the way.'

'How about that extra nurse?' Abby called to her departing back.

'She's on her way, too!'

'You, set up for the cyclist,' Abby ordered Haley, as the orthopaedic registrar flew through the door. 'I'll deal with the OD. Hopefully the security officers will stay and help!'

She wasn't joking! Making sure she had everything else to hand, Abby rechecked the drug Haley had drawn up, knowing that if this was indeed a heroin overdose, the man being carried in grey and lifeless by Security could very well turn into one angry young man indeed when his overdose was reversed.

'It's Pete,' Abby said as the young man was placed on the trolley beside her.

'I really thought he'd turned his life around after the last scare.'

'Ever the optimist,' Haley sighed as the orthopaedic registrar made his way over.

'My motorcyclist hasn't arrived yet, how about I lend a hand?'

He bagged the patient with essential oxygen as Abby struggled to find a vein in Pete's thin bruised arms. 'Got one,' she said finally on her third attempt. 'And not a moment too soon. It looks like your motorcyclist is here,' she commented as the blue lights of the ambulance flashed past the window. 'I'll be over to help when I can.' Picking up the syringe, Abby gave a thin smile to the two burly security guards. 'Ready, guys.'

The drug worked in seconds.

The young man, who only seconds before had been deeply unconscious and barely breathing, precariously close to death, suddenly attempted to sit up, cursing and swearing angrily, furious with the world.

'Hi, Pete,' Abby said in a resigned voice as the vile language continued. 'So you've come back to see us again.'

Even with their combined strength, the security officers were struggling to hold the young man down, and Abby stood back slightly as she spoke to him. 'You nearly died, Pete.'

'I'd have been fine.'

'No,' Abby said sharply. 'A couple of minutes more and you'd have been brain damaged, and a couple of minutes more than that and you'd have been dead. Now, I want you to calm down, and when you have, you and I are going to have a long talk.'

'You're wasting your time,' Pete shouted, struggling to sit up. 'What would you know?'

'Too much,' Abby said, meeting his eyes full on. 'I lost a dear friend because of drugs and I lose more patients than I can even bear to think about due to them, so I know plenty. Now, like it or not, Pete, I'm on your back, and for once you're going to listen to me.'

'Get lost,' Pete sneered.

'Settle down, mate.'

The calmest, most easygoing of voices, so out of place

in an emergency room, suddenly filled the air and Abby stared, just stared at the muscular, tanned forearm that was pushing Pete back down onto the trolley.

'I'd suggest you lie there and do what the doctor says, huh? It can't hurt to listen.'

Still her eyes didn't dare move. Instead, they stayed trained on Kell's arms, scrutinising every dark hair, the veins on the back of his hand, the neat white nails, terrified that if she moved if she blinked, if she even breathed, he might somehow disappear.

'What are you doing here?' She finally croaked, confused, overwhelmed but utterly, utterly delighted.

'Didn't the agency say I was coming?' Kell winked.

'*You're* the agency nurse?'

'A word, Abby, please?' Jane's none-too-dulcet tones wouldn't wait and with a bemused shake of her head Abby made to go, but her legs just wouldn't move.

'Go,' Kell said gently. 'We'll still be here when you get back, won't we, Pete?'

'I'm so sorry.' Jane grimaced as Abby came over. 'I never thought he'd just march in.'

'Who?'

'Kelvin. The agency's really overstretched the mark this time. He's a bush nurse—a bush nurse!' Jane repeated, shaking her head in disbelief. 'I told him there's no snakes here, young man, and I said he could try and make himself useful tidying the pan room and running a few patients up to the ward.'

'And what did he say?' Abby asked, a markedly absent smile forming on her lips.

'Well, that's just it. He just shrugged and carried right on over to resus, I honestly don't think he's the full ticket, and he's certainly not what I ordered from the agency.'

'His name's Kell, Jane, not Kelvin, and he's exactly what you ordered.'

'What do you mean?'

Abby was smiling now, really smiling as Jane stared at her, bemused. 'You need to loosen up a bit Jane. He's *everything* this department needs.'

He was, too.

On they worked, through this busy Saturday night, and nothing, not a single thing, fazed him. Flirting gently with the old ladies, chatting amicably with the drunks, making tea and toast for the down-and-outs one minute, performing cardiac massage on a teenager the next. Even the sex workers who trickled in tired and weary in the small hours of the morning perked up a bit when they saw Kell writing his notes at the nurses' station.

'Where did *that* come from?' Gloria, one of the regular sex workers, asked as Abby finished stitching her hand, gaping in open-mouthed admiration as Kell breezed into the theatre to check a drug with Jane.

'He's from the bush,' Jane said once Kell had gone, snipping Abby's suture, her voice growing more gushing by the minute. 'And despite my earlier doubts, he's an absolute treasure.'

'That'll be right,' Gloria muttered. 'They don't make men like that in the city.' Sitting up, she straightened her red boob tube and patted her curls. 'I could give him my card on the way out.' With a saucy wink she fished in her purse. 'I might even offer him a discount.'

'That won't be necessary, Gloria.' A distinctly proprietorial note came to Abby's voice as she pulled off her gloves and tossed them in the bin.

'What are you getting so uppity about?' Jane teased goodnaturedly as a wide grin split Gloria's face.

'I'd say your doctor is in love, Sister.' Gloria laughed,

stepping down off the trolley and attempting to straighten her inch of skirt. 'And if she's got any sense, she'd better do something about it!'

Abby found Kell in the staffroom, boots on the table, lounging on the sofa as if he came here every night.

'They really weren't talking about you, Abby,' he said with a smile as she came in. 'This coffee is seriously bad.'

'There's a jar of decent stuff in the kitchen.'

'I saw, but it also said it was the property of Abby Hampton and hands off.'

'Since when did that stop you?'

The joking was over now, the small talk had run out and Abby stood utterly still as he came over and put his arms around her, burying his head in her hair, breathing in the sweet smell as if it was the life force he depended upon.

'God, I've missed you. Don't ever, ever leave me like that again.'

'Oh, Kell.' She held him, held him so close, his skin, his smell, everything she missed, everything she needed. 'I just couldn't see how—'

'Hey.' He pulled her chin up gently. 'No getting upset. I'm here, aren't I? And Jane's already offered me a whole fortnight of shifts.'

'Don't, Kell.' She shook her head fiercely, determined to get in first, to counter his temporary solution with a permanent one. 'You told me the first night we met you could never leave Tennengarrah, and I can't be cross at you because I felt the same. You'll end up resenting me—'

'Abby.' His voice broke in, that lazy, lazy smile halting her in her tracks. 'That was the first night I met you—before I'd held you, tasted you, made love to you. You can't hold me accountable for what I said then.'

'You love it there, Kell. I can't ask you to leave.'

'You haven't,' Kell pointed out. 'I've made that choice all by myself. You running away like that has taken me to hell and back, but in other ways it's been exactly what I needed. Tennengarrah's got its charms and I love it, yes, but without you, Abby, it just felt empty. Maybe I needed that time without you to realise that I *could* leave, to see what really mattered to me.' He let his words sink in, staring down at her with love blazing from his eyes as his voice imbued her with long-forgotten hope. 'You know when they say, ''Love will find a way.'' Have you ever stopped to think what that means?'

'It's all I've thought about,' she admitted, one shaking hand retrieving the letter, watching his face for a reaction as he read it, watching the wonder in his eyes when he finally looked up.

'You'd give it all up for me?'

She nodded slowly but with absolute certainty. 'You don't have to leave, Kell. All I'm asking is that you wait a year for me.'

'No.' Her eyes shot up at his answer, confusion turning to wonder as Kell carried on talking. 'We don't have to wait, Abby. I'm not letting you out of my sight ever again. I'm coming to live here, with no hang-ups, no resentment, because, quite simply, I love you. You're a consultant, for heaven's sake, a consultant with a crazy dream about saving the world, and the most amazing part of it is that I'm starting to think you could do it.'

'I'm hardly going to save the world,' Abby countered. 'This programme will barely scratch the surface.'

'It's a start, though,' Kell said gently. 'And who

knows where it will lead? This is where you belong, Abby. I'm not going to punish you for that. I just want to be with you.'

Hope flared deep inside and she waited, waited for it to be doused, for the ifs or buts that would surely come, a demand, a condition, a time span that would surely render the problem insurmountable. But black eyes just kept on smiling, and those strong arms moved around her as he fumbled in his pocket and pulled out the ring she'd been so scared to glimpse.

'It's an Argyle diamond,' Kell said as she stared in wonder at the massive pink diamond glinting back at her, set high on a delicate gold band. 'I know you're probably not one for pink, but I saw the stone and I just fell in love with it—rare and unique like you, and from the heart of Australia like me.' He slipped it onto her shaking hand as she stared at it in bemused wonder.

'Are you sure, Kell, I mean, really sure? This is such a huge step, Tennengarrah's in your blood...' The last question slipped out of her mouth, needing to be voiced and, more importantly, needing to be answered.

'Tennengarrah's in my blood,' he interrupted, then planted the softest, gentlest of kisses on her mouth before he finished, before it was Kell's turn to put the world to rights...

'But you, Abby, you're in my heart.'

Modern Romance™
...seduction and
passion guaranteed

Tender Romance™
...love affairs that
last a lifetime

Medical Romance™
...medical drama
on the pulse

Historical Romance™
...rich, vivid and
passionate

Sensual Romance™
...sassy, sexy and
seductive

Blaze Romance™
...the temperature's
rising

27 new titles every month.

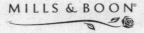

MILLS & BOON®

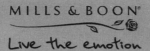

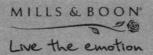

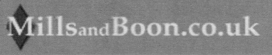

4 FREE

books and a surprise gift!

We would like to take this opportunity to thank you for reading this Mills & Boon® book by offering you the chance to take FOUR more specially selected titles from the Medical Romance™ series absolutely FREE! We're also making this offer to introduce you to the benefits of the Reader Service™—

- ★ FREE home delivery
- ★ FREE gifts and competitions
- ★ FREE monthly Newsletter
- ★ Exclusive Reader Service offers
- ★ Books available before they're in the shops

Accepting these FREE books and gift places you under no obligation to buy, you may cancel at any time, even after receiving your free shipment. Simply complete your details below and return the entire page to the address below. *You don't even need a stamp!*

YES! Please send me 4 free Medical Romance books and a surprise gift. I understand that unless you hear from me, I will receive 6 superb new titles every month for just £2.60 each, postage and packing free. I am under no obligation to purchase any books and may cancel my subscription at any time. The free books and gift will be mine to keep in any case.

M4ZED

Ms/Mrs/Miss/Mr ....Initials......................................
BLOCK CAPITALS PLEASE

Surname ....

Address ....

....

....Postcode...................................

Send this whole page to:
UK: FREEPOST CN81, Croydon, CR9 3WZ
EIRE: PO Box 4546, Kilcock, County Kildare (stamp required)